HUNTED

THE IMMORTAL ONES - BOOK THREE

Shade Owens

PROLOGUE

I sat with my back against the cold wall, wishing I'd never entered this place.

Countless young children shivered, their bottom lips trembling as they held on to their parents.

What had I done?

The air was cool and damp as if the entire room were sitting at the bottom of the ocean. Everywhere I looked, concrete walls ran up to meet the high ceiling. In the middle of the large room stood massive columns that started from the floor and connected to the ceiling. What were those things? Support posts? On the ceiling that seemed to never end were white circular lights that reminded me of stars across a cloudless night sky.

Men dressed in black patrolled the area while eyeing us from behind shielded faces. When someone moved—even if only to reposition themselves—one of the men aimed a large gun at them, threatening to blow off their head.

"I'm scared," came a tiny voice.

"It's okay, sweetheart," the mother said. She brushed her son's hair away from his sticky forehead and kissed the top of his head.

"Keep your mouth shut!" shouted the nearest man in black.

"He's only a child," the mother said.

The man stomped his way over to her, twirled his gun around, and smashed her in the face with it. She cried out, and blood splattered out of her nose and across her holey, floral shirt.

A man sitting next to her jumped to his feet, prepared to attack the man in black, when a loud sound exploded all around us. I didn't understand what was happening at first. Yet the sound was so loud that I slapped my hands over my ears, which did nothing. Although it muffled the loud sound, a loud, persistent ringing echoed in my head.

Then, I saw it.

My heart sank as I watched the horrific scene unfold before me. People shook violently as bullets penetrated their chests and blood splashed from the backs and onto the wall. I couldn't tell if they were convulsing or if the bullets were making their bodies jerk so wildly.

I'd never seen anyone get shot before.

I'd never seen... a massacre.

I froze, watching everyone I'd come to know as my people get killed at the hands of these strange men. My heart pounded so hard I began to wonder if I was even alive. Maybe I was dead, because this was too awful to be real.

I blinked hard, hoping to wake up, but every time I opened my eyes, more people were dead—piled atop each other with blood soaking into their clothes and into the concrete underneath them.

Then, the guns were turned on me.

CHAPTER 1

S ilver."

"No, please," I cried.

I didn't feel the pain at first. What I felt was my back crashing into the concrete wall behind me and warm blood spilling down my spine.

"Silver!"

Searing pain hit me at last. I'd been shot in the ribs. Reaching for my abdomen, I touched something wet and warm.

"Silver!"

Another slew of bullets fired through the air, and my body thrashed violently. I wanted to scream—ask them to stop—but I couldn't speak. Everything was happening too fast.

"Silver!"

My body shook one last time before Sadie's face appeared inches away from mine. She scowled at me, her brows so close together they looked like a single brow. She shook me again. "Wake up!"

Slowly, my surroundings came into focus.

Although everything looked the same—concrete walls and columns all around me—there were no men in black with shielded faces, and no one had been shot. Instead, everyone sat against the walls quietly. Some people slept, while others held on to each other, sharing stories and discussing their fears.

I searched the open space until I found the man who had let us inside this place. He stood a bit farther up the ramp we had descended and next to Finn. Behind him was the large door through which we'd entered during the storm.

What was this place? The bunker we'd been searching for? And where were we now? The entrance? This place was humongous, so vast that it easily fit our four carriages and hundreds of people. I stared at the man as he spoke with Finn, wondering what they were talking about. Reina soon joined them, nodding and pointing at the main entrance.

This man had saved our lives.

"You okay?" Sadie asked.

She winced, grabbed her side, and slowly lowered herself next to me. She didn't look so good herself. Her skin was pale, but at least she could keep her eyes open longer than five minutes.

Nodding, I searched the room. Across from us—at the opposite end of this tunnel—were more people sitting against the wall. I could see shoes, bare feet, and a few young faces lying on their parents' laps, but the horses and carts stationed at the center of the room made it impossible to see anything else.

I followed the ramp down to where it ended. At the back wall were four metallic doors, all of which seemed thick and impenetrable.

Would we be allowed to enter through them?

Next to the doors and along the opposing wall was another large door that reminded me of the ones in the Receiving area of Olympus—the type of door that was pulled up into the ceiling by a cable.

Would the man allow our carriages through that door?

One of the regular-sized doors suddenly opened and out came three men and two women carrying shiny guns. They held on to them firmly, their footsteps echoing throughout the space as they marched toward us.

Same as I'd seen in my nightmare, the guards were dressed in black from head to toe, with hard-looking pads protecting their shoulders, elbows, and knees.

I swallowed hard. "Who are those guys?"

Sadie pointed lazily at them. "Those guys? They keep coming in and out. Probably to make sure we don't try anything stupid. Not that we can. We left our weapons outside."

The tornado, I remembered.

Had it swept up all our weapons?

Armed guards with hardened features moved about. The one nearest to me had pale white skin that looked like snow against his tan shirt. A dark beard, as dark as his coal-colored eyes, masked the lower half of his face. His shoulders, broad and wide, stuck out far on either side of him as if he were trying to make himself look bigger.

He probably was.

Out of the bunch, this one made me feel like if things got out of control, he'd be the first to use his strength against anyone causing trouble.

In front of him and on either side of the carts were two dark-skinned men. Although scrawnier than the bearded one, these two were tall, lanky, and seemed to know how to handle their guns. I didn't want any trouble, but I also didn't want to feel threatened by them.

As Finn continued talking with the man in charge, Reina nodded and placed her hands on her waist. She then watched her shoes, like she was upset about something but was biting her tongue.

"I'll be back," I said, pushing myself up onto my feet.

Sadie reached for me, but she wasn't quick enough. "What? Where are you going?"

Ignoring her voice behind me, I moved toward Finn.

At the same time, the bearded man aimed a thick finger at me. "No one gets up. Sit down!"

His voice came out as more of a growl, bouncing off every wall inside the tunnel. All eyes turned on me as I froze, torn between wanting to ignore the command and continue my way over to Finn, and wanting to sit back down to avoid making my nightmare a reality.

As much as I hated being ordered around, I knew better.

Right as I took a step back, Finn called out, "Silver, it's okay. Come."

He gestured me to join him farther down the tunnel. The man with the beard gave me a sour look as I walked past him like he was pissed off for having been overruled by a stranger. He glared at his leader, but the leader shook his head as a way of saying, *Let the girl go.*

I avoided eye contact with the armed man and approached Finn and the others. When I drew in close, Finn extended an arm toward the man who had saved us. "Silver, this is Elias."

Elias tipped his brown hat at me.

Elias, I thought. I'd never heard that name before. He reached his hand out and shook mine. His grip was warm and firm, which made me feel weak and fragile.

When Finn caught my stare, he said, "I was just telling Elias about the Elites and our enemies and how we were attacked."

He paused, his gaze lingering on me like he was trying to communicate something to me telepathically. What was he trying to tell me? To keep my mouth shut about my background? About who I was and why the Woodfaces were after me?

It was my only guess. So I nodded politely but didn't say a word.

"Elias has been very generous in offering us shelter while the storm passes," Finn said.

The conversation felt strained, like Finn was trying extra hard to be polite to this man. Was it because our lives depended on it? Was he dangerous?

"You will be given some food before you go," Elias said.

He stared at me meaningfully, his dark eyes looking black compared to Finn's.

"Before we go?" I blurted. "We're going back out there?"

Both Finn and Reina raised their brows, warning me to keep my mouth shut.

Elias smiled at me as if I were nothing but an innocent child. "You have to understand, Silver. We have our own people to protect inside this bunker. We can't bring in anyone else. We have limited resources, limited power. I'm sure you understand."

My heart raced as I thought about going back into the open field, walking around blindly in search of a safe space to claim as our own. We'd come out this way looking for this bunker—for a place to call home. And now, after having stepped foot inside, we were being asked to leave.

I knew why Finn and Reina were so on edge about the whole thing—they understood what it meant to run a village. These strangers, whether they were good or bad, would do anything to protect their people. The only choice we had was to respect their wishes. Otherwise, blood would spill.

"Are you sure there isn't a way for us to work this out?" I asked.

Both Finn and Reina fidgeted, likely getting nervous with how persistent I was being.

"We've already tried discussing—" Finn said, but Elias cut him off.

"I'm certain." His gaze became cold—threatening, even. "The truth is, we don't know you. Allowing you inside my home could mean the death of my people. You should consider yourselves lucky that I even opened the gates for you."

Deep down, I knew he wasn't wrong. Had I been in his position, I wouldn't have wanted hundreds of strangers living with us inside of Ortus. Grandma had always taught me that people were dangerous. Even those who smiled in your face and offered to help could later stab you in the back—sometimes literally.

"Human beings are complex creatures," she'd once told me. "A concoction of unknown history, trauma, belief systems, and ethics. You can never trust anyone. Do you hear me?"

"I can trust you," I'd said.

She smiled sweetly and rubbed my cheek. "Only me."

"I understand," I finally said to Elias.

He tipped his hat at me again, dark curls dangling over his forehead, and offered me a half smile. He didn't look mean, but it was like he'd said—we didn't know one another. Maybe if we'd met under different circumstances, he'd have been less cold with us. But the fact that he'd allowed us inside, even if only for a few hours to save our lives, told me he was a good person.

A bad person would have let us die and later scavenged our bodies for supplies.

Elias's smile grew a bit wider, and he gave me a sweet look that made me think he had children of his own. "We have fresh bread, fruits, vegetables. We're happy to share some food with you before you go. I'll also give you a few bags of wheat and rice for your travels."

Finn nodded, holding his injured arm despite it resting in a sling. Then, he readjusted his weight against his staff. "That would be very much appreciated. Thank you, Elias."

CHAPTER 2

The young men and women avoided eye contact as they came in through the big metal door on the back wall. With them, they brought wooden carts with large wheels, the smooth rolling sound reverberating throughout the tunnel.

As the scent of fresh bread crept through the air, people sat upright—even the sickly and injured—and moaned and licked their lips. Most people became animated and excited, while a few others looked leery. Could they sense what was going on? Did they know it would only be a matter of time before Finn announced we couldn't stay here?

And when that time came, what would happen? Would the people lash out? Demand that we stay? We couldn't. This wasn't our land. Others had claimed this bunker and made a home for themselves. If we tried to take it, that made us the enemy... the bad guys.

I joined Sadie's side again, the concrete feeling like wet stone against my back as I sat down.

"Everything okay? What happened?"

I shook my head as a way of saying, *I don't want to talk about it right now.*

She seemed to understand. When a young girl no older than ten came by with a platter of bread rolls, Sadie beamed at her and grabbed two. With a slight bow of her head, the girl walked away, her white dress dragging on the floor behind her. This was the most I'd seen Sadie smile since I'd met her. What did she have to be so happy about? Did she love kids? Or was she still being affected by whatever medicine they'd given her?

When she caught me staring, her features hardened. "What?" she demanded

I smirked, took one of the rolls from her, and bit into it. "Nothing."

Warm butter spilled from the corners of my mouth. The bread tasted fresh and felt fluffy against my tongue. They must have taken them fresh out of the oven for us.

Ovens, I thought.

If they had ovens, they had electricity, like the Elites.

How else would they have made this food?

My gaze shifted toward the overhead lights and the automatic door through which more food carts were coming.

Maybe we could find an abandoned city and learn to regenerate power. The thought of going back out there after we were lucky enough to end up here made my stomach churn. Who was to say that next time we'd be so lucky?

I wanted to tell Sadie what Elias had told me, but I didn't want anyone to overhear me. Still, she knew something was up.

After I finished my bread, I swallowed hard, and a young boy came by, offering us drinks. He leaned forward, handing each person a little paper cup with water up to the brim. Everyone grabbed it—some more aggressively than others—and chugged it back.

Slowly, I sipped the water, appreciating its cold and crisp taste. Once finished, I crumpled the little cone in my fist and stared at it as a bead of water dripped through the crack of my thumb and down my wrist.

"Something's wrong," Sadie said.

As she spoke, several eyes turned on me. I wanted to tell her to stop bothering me about it, but Sadie was worried, and she had every right to be.

Shaking my head, I forced a smile. "Just tired."

She didn't believe me. Why would she? But she didn't question me on it again, likely sensing that others were listening.

Suddenly, the doors at the back wall blasted open, and in came a tall, slim man with black hair, pale skin, and an aggressive walk that told me he was ready to rip someone's head off. He glowered at all of us as he walked in. Behind him, men dressed in black uniforms followed him with balled fists, and I swallowed hard.

Although they didn't look exactly like the men in my dreams, their anger did.

"What's the meaning of this, brother?" shouted the slim man.

His voice carried down the tunnel to Elias, capturing his attention. Elias said something to Finn, touched his shoulder, and started walking toward his brother. He walked past grunting pigs and nervous cows, petting one of them on the back as he went.

"Let's speak in private, Jared," Elias said as he drew in closer.

Although they looked alike, with dark features and curly hair, there was a softness to Elias that his brother didn't have.

Jared stomped forward with heavy black boots, spread them at shoulder's width, and crossed his arms. The six men behind him did the same, scowling just as hard.

"How can you share our rations with strangers?" Jared hissed. "Have you lost your mind? There must be at least"—he searched the tunnel with his beady eyes—"hundreds of them. And then the animals! Unless we're taking them for meat."

I clenched a fist, prepared to give him a piece of my mind, when Sadie's warm grip caught me by surprise. She shook her head and gave me a warning look that said, *Let's wait and see how this plays out.*

"When our people find out about this—" Jared started.

"My people," Elias corrected, "are good people. And they'll understand me wanting to save other human beings. These travelers were targeted by a group of outlaws. They lost everything."

Jared scoffed like he was amused by his brother's empathy. "That's not our problem and you know it."

"I'm not having this discussion here," Elias said. "Get out."

"I suppose you're letting them stay, too," Jared said. "Giving them warm beds. Letting them share the little food that we have." He turned to his men and laughed; they chuckled like a bunch of idiots.

"What I choose to do is none of your concern," Elias said.

Jared's features suddenly hardened, his square jaw popping out on both sides. "That's where you're wrong!" He jabbed a finger in

Elias's face. "When you were sworn in, no one agreed to a dictatorship. The people will never agree to this!"

Elias stuck a thumb out away from his brother. "Get him out of here."

At once, his armed men and women moved toward Jared and the others, threatening them with their guns.

"Pointing guns at your own brother, Elias. Really?" Jared scoffed. Reaching down, he tore a piece of bread right out of an old woman's hands. He sank his teeth into it, chewed like a wild animal, and swallowed hard. He then shook the bread at Elias. "This belongs to us. Not them. And you'd better remember that."

He threw the rest of it on the ground and jerked his head sideways, ordering his men to follow him.

The moment the doors closed shut behind him, people began bickering in a panic.

"Are we not staying here?"

"I thought we were safe!"

"They're going to kick us out."

"Do you really want to stay here with a bunch of armed guards?"

"Enough!" Reina shouted, and everyone went quiet. She turned to Finn and Elias, whispering.

What were they saying? What was happening? I got up, despite Sadie trying to stop me again, and rushed over to Finn and Reina.

"We can't go out there," I blurted, and Reina made her eyes go big at me.

"Sit down, Silver," she ordered.

"We have no food," I said. "And the Woodfaces could be waiting out there. We have no idea where they are, or if they saw us migrating before the storm hit."

Elias's nose crinkled. "*Woodfaces?*"

Several people behind me gasped and footsteps shuffled. It was like the mere expression of our enemy's name was enough to send everyone into a panic again.

"Um, sir," came a woman's voice in the distance.

"Silver's right," someone said. "We can't go out there."

"What are these Woodfaces?" Elias asked, squinting at me. "Are those the enemies Finn spoke about?"

"Sir," the same voice repeated.

Several heads turned to the blond woman calling for Elias. Like Elias's other armed followers, the woman wore a black uniform and stood with a straight back. Although far away from us, it was apparent she was a large woman—easily Elias's height, if not taller. She stood at the front of the entrance, pointing at a strange machine secured to the wall. It was surrounded by buttons, lights, and little wires. She mouthed something, then urged Elias to come forward.

Elias and Finn exchanged a worried look before walking hastily toward the woman at the front door. The moment they reached her side, Elias grabbed the contraption on the wall and moved his face into it, resting his forehead against the metal structure.

When he pulled away, a menacing scowl formed on his face. It was so threatening that I clenched my fists, prepared to defend Finn. He said something to Finn, and although I couldn't hear it from this distance, it looked like an accusation.

Finn shook his head, seemingly confused by Elias's words.

Elias jabbed the machine and then Finn's chest, ordering him to look through it.

Finn did as he was told, and as he stared through the machine, he brought his uninjured arm up and ran a hand through his chestnut hair. I'd seen Finn do this enough times to know it meant he was uneasy.

"They brought them here!" said the blond woman.

Elias turned sharply her way and hissed something, but it was too late. Everyone in the tunnel had heard the blond woman's voice, and one by one, people began to stand.

"What's going on?" I said.

Reina gave me a big-eyed look that told me I was out of line for getting involved, but I didn't care. I'd gotten everyone inside this tunnel, so it only felt natural that I be involved in whatever problem we were facing.

"An army is approaching," Elias said, matter-of-factly.

His features had softened, which told me he was fighting with himself not to accuse us of being responsible. But every few seconds, his nostrils flared and he shot Finn a hateful glare.

I looked at Finn, prepared to ask him what he'd seen, when he said, "It's the Woodfaces."

Everyone behind me gasped and shuffled their feet.

I stared at Elias. "But we're safe here, aren't we?"

"Safe?" Elias repeated, his tone harsh and demeaning. "We may have thick walls, but this threat could endanger the lives of *my* people!"

Although I didn't appreciate his aggressive demeanor, I understood Elias's concern. His top priority was his people—not us. Allowing us to enter his home had been a favor, nothing more. He didn't owe us anything, especially not a battle against our enemies.

"How did they follow you?" Elias asked. His dark eyes turned into little black slits that made him look like his brother Jared.

"I-I don't know," Finn admitted. "There could have been a few following us in the forest. They must have waited for the storm to pass."

"There are hundreds out there," Elias growled.

"Aren't these walls impenetrable?" Finn asked.

The question itself was perfectly reasonable. But Elias didn't seem to appreciate Finn's nonchalant response. He sucked in a sharp breath and held it as if it would prevent him from slaying Finn with words.

Eventually, he blew back out, grabbed his hips, and bowed his head. I couldn't tell if he was at a loss for words, or if he was trying hard not to yell at Finn.

"If these enemies of yours know you're in here, it means they saw the door open," he said. "We may be safe underground, but we have an outside courtyard several miles from here. We also have solar panels around our perimeter. If they're damaged—"

"We'll make sure they aren't," said the blond woman who spotted the Woodfaces in the first place.

"Sofia," Elias said, trying to stay calm. "This isn't our fight—"

"What choice do we have, sir?" the woman

asked. "These people are threatening our land, which now makes them *our* enemy."

A few more armed men and women stepped forward, listening in on the conversation. Elias paused, watching them carefully.

Was he preparing to give an attack order? After all, his people had guns. The Woodfaces didn't. Surely, the fight wouldn't last long. Slowly, his gaze shifted to us.

"What doesn't make sense to me is why an entire army would follow you for miles," he said. "Armies don't do that. People don't do that. Not unless they're after something. And most wars are for territory. So unless they're coming here for our bunker, your story doesn't add up." He paused and watched Finn carefully. "Wars happen because of disagreements. For all I know, you people attacked first."

"We didn't," Finn said sharply. "We had a treaty with these people and they broke it."

Elias elevated his head, the brim of his hat aimed at the concrete ceiling. "And why would they do that?"

His accusatory tone led some of his followers to point their guns at us.

Finn raised his hands on either side of him. "Is that necessary?"

"I don't know," Elias said. "You tell me."

I much preferred the kind version of Elias

from earlier—the one who had defended us against his brother. But Elias was clearly in charge of this place, which meant he had to take every precaution. He was also a smart man who knew we were hiding something.

"They're after me," I blurted.

"Silver!" Finn hissed.

Elias's lips broke into a smile. He took off his hat again, and started waving it between Finn and me as he spoke. "Oh, I get it. Some sort of father-daughter relationship here, right? And you're trying to protect her."

It was apparent that he was getting impatient, and I didn't blame him. Nobody liked being lied to.

"He's not my father," I said. "My father lives in Olympus."

Elias's eyes widened. "Olympus?"

"It's a long story," I said. "I'm from Lutum."

His eyes got even wider.

"I was offered the serum and I rejected it. Long story short, the Elites are after me. So, if you want this to be over, just throw me out of here and the Woodfaces will leave your people alone."

Behind me, rapid footsteps approached.

"Silver, what are you doing?" Sadie hissed.

She shuffled through the crowd, pushing people aside despite her fragile state. Elias watched her as she stepped forward, staring hatefully his way.

The room went quiet and Elias watched longer than necessary. "Let me get this straight... You all knew they were after her"—he pointed at me with a stiff finger—"and you risked war over giving her up?"

One by one, the people of Ortus nodded.

"Why?" Elias made a sour face. "Why would you risk all of your lives for one person?"

Sadie clenched her fists. "It isn't for one person." She looked sideways at me, then at Finn. "It's an idea. It's hope. Silver helps us stay brave."

I wasn't sure how I helped anyone stay brave, but I was happy to hear it.

Elias slowly raised his chin. "These enemies of yours... The Woodfaces, as you call them... Will they stop once they have you?"

His gaze was on me now. Sadie took another step toward him, her jaw muscles popping. I reached for her arm, stopping her from going any farther. If he wanted to throw me out, maybe it was for the best. Inside, my heart thudded hard, but I wouldn't show anyone how scared I was. I didn't want people to know I was panicking. Of course, I didn't want to be handed over to our enemies. There was no telling what they would do to me. Worse, what would the Elites do after everything I'd put them through?

"Yes," I said. "They'll stop. The Elites want *me*."

"We don't know that for sure," Finn said. "They may very well choose to punish all of us for taking you in."

Bickering broke out inside the concrete tunnel, until eventually, Elias raised a hand and everyone went quiet.

"I have no intention of letting you go out there without any means to protect yourselves," he said.

This took me by surprise. I breathed out slowly, trying to keep my knees from trembling.

Elias bowed his head, then breathed out through flared nostrils. "My parents came from Lutum." He paused and took in a deep breath. "I know how bad it is. During their escape, the Elites stopped and killed my mother. My father led me and my brother as far away from there as possible. If these Woodfaces are working for the Elites, we'll help you fight them... but under one condition."

Everyone stared intently.

"You help us fight the Elites," Elias said. "We have strong weapons, but not enough people."

Finn hesitated. Elias didn't know that Finn was technically an Elite—or at least, that he *used* to be. Nor that his wife and daughter were still inside Olympus.

"They're not all bad," Finn said. "There are innocent people within those walls."

Elias smiled like he was holding back a scoff.

"He's right," I said. "I was in Olympus. Children are being used as slaves. They're forced to work until they reach eighteen. They're guarded by Defenders like we were, in Lutum. And if they step out of line, they're punished. Killed, even."

Elias's dark eyes lingered on me like he was trying to figure out whether I was making it up.

"She's telling the truth," came Dax's voice.

Dax stepped forward, slightly taller than Sadie, and crossed her muscular arms over her chest. Beside her was Danika, who pulled her red hair over one shoulder and smiled sweetly at me, offering silent support. Rose soon emerged from the crowd, silent as always. But the look on her dark face told me she was willing to put up a fight if necessary.

These women knew firsthand how Olympus operated. They'd spent years as Breeders within its walls, whereas I'd only been there a few days to witness the injustices. I imagined there was more that I knew nothing about.

"We can find a way to defeat the Elites without killing everyone inside," Finn said.

Elias pondered this for a second, scratched

at his beard, and extended his hand to Finn.
"Deal."

CHAPTER 3

Gather our soldiers," Elias ordered. "On my signal, I want a tank team on that army."

Two of his armed men nodded and jogged for the back doors in the tunnel.

Elias spun around. "Sofia, what's your update?"

Sofia leaned into the strange gadget and stood with a rounded back for several seconds, then pulled away. "They're gathering closer. They have"—she paused, seemingly concentrating—"bows, swords, spears, batons."

"No artillery?" Elias asked.

"Negative," Sofia said. "At least, none that I can see."

"You can't open those doors!" shouted an old man, wagging a finger at Elias. "They'll kill us. We ain't got no weapons!"

Elias, keeping a calm demeanor, smiled at

the man. "Don't worry, sir. I have no intention of opening this door. We'll be taking care of them."

People whispered, most of them sounding fearful of the Woodfaces.

One woman brushed her daughter's hair behind her shoulders and said, "Don't worry, sweetheart. See these walls? They're as strong as your father. No one is coming down here to hurt us, okay?"

The little girl nodded, rubbing a hand across her grimy face. Her bottom lip trembled as she fought back tears.

"We're going to be fine," I told her, smiling.

Her lips stopped trembling, and even her mother smiled back. It was as if my words had been enough to ease both their minds. A few others nodded at me like they were thanking me for consoling them.

As more and more people looked to me for guidance, I felt like they were waiting for something. Did they want more? Did they need to hear me tell everyone that we would come out of this victorious? I turned to Finn, hoping he might step in and reassure everyone as the leader of Ortus. Instead, he nudged his chin, encouraging me to speak.

I looked around the dimly lit space as several big eyes watched me. Some people trembled, others winced in pain as they held on to their injured limbs. We were a wreck—all of us. We'd survived war, and we'd survived a tornado.

"We didn't go through all of that just to die," I said.

Those who had been watching me with big eyes became even more animated. My words had taken them by surprise.

"You people are the strongest people I've ever met," I continued. "In Lutum, everyone is a coward." I felt uncomfortable, like I didn't belong at the back of the tunnel, delivering some speech. But it was obvious by the way they were staring at me that they wanted to hear me talk. After all the lives that had been laid down to protect mine, I owed them that, at the very least. "I don't mean to say they're bad people. We were raised to be cowards. The people of Lutum are trained by the Elites and the Defenders to be afraid to take a stand. You *aren't*." I paused. "That makes you the true heroes."

Lips parted and the sound of throats clearing spread throughout the tunnel.

No one knew what to say to that.

"You might think of me as some hero, but I'm no different from you. I'm not some warrior who took a stand against the Elites. I politely declined the serum because the lottery was a tie and I preferred to stay with my family. For some reason, that angered the Elites."

"That's not what we heard," someone whispered.

"Yeah, me neither," someone else said.

"I'm sorry if the story got embellished by the time it reached you," I said. "That's usually what happens when stories travel."

A warm hand suddenly rested on my shoulder, and Finn leaned into me. "You don't have to do this."

I pulled away. "I want to."

I bowed my head, remembering all the faces in Lutum as I delivered my fake speech— the one professing to them how *happy* I was in Olympus. Again, I'd done it to save my family, yet I felt guilt at having lied to so many people.

"I even lied to my own people to save my family," I said.

A young woman around my age scowled at me. "So what? Anyone else would have done the same thing."

"Yeah!" someone shouted.

I was grateful for their support, but it wasn't the reason for my speech. I wanted these people to know the truth. If they were going to keep fighting on my behalf, they deserved to know who I truly was.

"If you choose to keep fighting," I said, "don't do it for me, because I'm not the one who's going to lead you to victory. Only *you* can do that. Do it for the people of Lutum. For your family. Your loved ones. That's what you should be fighting for. That's what I'm fighting for."

Nods spread throughout the crowd. A few people held solid fists in the air as a sign of solidarity, while others, seemingly exhausted, simply offered a faint smile.

"But today, we aren't fighting," I said. "You've already done so much, and I can't thank you enough for the bravery you've shown. We're safe down here"—I pointed at the walls around us, then at Elias. "And because of this man, we get to live another day."

"Elias," Sofia said suddenly.

Elias rushed to Sofia's side and pressed his face into the viewing instrument—something I'd earlier heard Elias refer to as a *periscope.*

"Who is that?" Elias asked.

Sofia shook her head. "I don't know, sir."

"What's going on?" someone asked.

Elias didn't respond. Instead, he looked to Finn. "Do you know this woman?"

Finn pressed his face into the viewing port but pulled away and shook his head. "I've never seen her before."

Next, Elias turned to me. I rushed to the periscope and peered inside. The view was strange. The color was faded and darker in the corners. Across the entire view was a giant cross—thin black lines that met at the center.

It took me a few seconds to adjust to the strange sight, but it wasn't long before I saw her.

But... how?

"That's Asako!" I said.

Rapid footsteps sounded behind me, but I didn't pull away. I wanted to keep looking. Asako knelt in the grass with her head bowed and her hands tied behind her back. Behind her stood a broad-shouldered Woodface carrying what looked like a metal sword. He stood tall with the sword resting on her shoulder. It was a stance that told me he was waiting to hear from us before deciding whether or not to slice the sword through her neck.

"What is he doing?" I asked.

"Threatening you," Elias said.

When I finally pulled away, Dax, Danika, and Rose stood next to me.

"Let me see," Dax said.

Without waiting for Elias's permission, she nudged me aside and peered into the periscope. "That's her. That's Asako!"

Danika was next, urging Dax to step out of the way.

Rose waited quietly for her turn, fidgeting with her thumbs. When she looked, she gasped but didn't say a word.

"Why are we all just standing here?" Dax growled. Her dark brows came together and she searched us one by one, waiting for someone to say something.

"What are we supposed to do?" Danika said. "Either way, someone loses their life."

"What's that supposed to mean?" Dax asked, towering over her.

"They're doing this because they want Silver," Reina cut in. "They're threatening you with one of your friends."

"Open the communication lines," Elias ordered.

Sofia reached for a button, then flipped a switch. A loud, staticky noise filled the space around us. It sounded like wind—fragmented and high-pitched.

Sofia stared at Elias, waiting for her next command.

Elias paused and looked at me. "Tell them we'll give them what they want. We'll give them Silver."

CHAPTER 4

You son of a bitch!" Finn swung a tight fist at Elias's jaw, but right before impact, Elias swept his face to the side, dodging the attack.

In one swift motion, Elias grabbed Finn by the collar of his shirt and pinned him against the concrete wall, nearly smashing him into a bunch of buttons and wires. More and more of our people rushed forward with balled fists and tight lips. Although we didn't have any weapons, it was apparent that our Champions had no issue with close combat.

Next to us, Elias's soldiers raised their guns, and clicking sounds filled the room.

Finn's face darkened three shades of red as Elias held him firmly in place. Reina fidgeted, likely wanting to get involved, but she knew better. I wondered if Finn would have better defended himself if he weren't injured. Elias wasn't as tall as Finn, but he was thick and seemed strong. His biceps bulged at the edge of his white T-shirt's sleeve, and several veins popped out of his tan, hairy arm.

"Let me make something perfectly clear to you," Elias said. "Down here, I'm in charge. You don't question my ways. In case you forgot, we made a deal. I gave you my word that I would help you defeat your enemies if you helped us take down the Elites. Have you forgotten that?"

Finn stared at him with such hatred that I wondered if he was planning to take another swing.

"I remember," Finn growled.

"And I'm a man of my word," Elias said, his brown leather boots nearly crushing Finn's toes. "If you'd trusted me, we could have avoided this altercation."

"You crossed us," Finn said.

Elias gave Finn a small smile as though amused by his anger. "Crossed you? How did I cross you?"

"You're giving Silver up—"

Elias brought his face close to Finn's, his nostrils flaring. I was surprised his hat didn't hit Finn's forehead. "I'm not giving her up. I'm buying us time. You need to take a step back, calm down, and use your words next time you need me to clarify something for you."

Finn didn't respond.

The air was tense as the soldiers waited,

their weapons on all of us.

"Lower your weapons," Elias ordered, still staring at Finn. "This is between me and him, not the people."

Finn and Elias stared at each other for what felt like minutes, until finally, Elias said, "Are you good?"

The redness in Finn's face diminished. He cleared his throat and nodded. "I'm good."

Elias let him go and Finn readjusted his shirt.

I felt bad for Finn, having been pinned against a wall in front of all his people. But on the flip side, he'd tried to punch the leader of this bunker in front of *his* people.

Sofia waited tensely, eyeballing the small speaker on the control panel. "Sir?"

"Go ahead, tell them," Elias said, his stare lingering on Finn.

He must have been anticipating another swing to the jaw.

Sofia leaned into the speaker, the small blond bun at the back of her head chafing against the collar of her shirt. "We have someone you want," she said, matter-of-factly.

Elias moved to the periscope, watching as Sofia spoke.

Then, through the speakers came a loud yet distant-sounding voice. It was grainy, and forced, making me picture a large man with a disfigured face and a long black beard. I didn't know what the Woodface looked like under his mask, but I imagined it was intimidating. "Silverstasia Blackwood!"

"Let the woman go and we will open the doors to release Silver," Sofia said.

There was a moment of silence as wind whistled through the speaker.

Sofia released the button and turned to Elias. "Are they letting her go?"

Elias peered into the periscope. "No, not yet."

"Release Silverstasia first!" His voice sounded like crushed stones rolling over a sheet of metal.

Sofia hesitated, waiting for Elias's instructions. He pulled away from the periscope, scratched his short beard pensively, and said, "They want her more than we want this woman. They have no advantage."

Suddenly, after we heard another staticky voice nearby, one of Elias's men spoke into a little black gadget. He nodded, pressed a button, and spoke. "Confirmed." Turning his attention to Elias, he added, "Sir, our troops are prepared to exit."

"Not yet," Elias said. "We need the girl away from the army. If we start firing now, we risk killing her."

Elias pointed at Finn, ordering him to watch

the periscope, then approached the communications area. He leaned forward and pressed the same button Sofia had held her thumb over. "This is Elias Gray, leader of the Ford Denton. You have precisely ten seconds to release the girl before we fire devastating blasts at your entire army. We have guns, ammunition, and plenty of grenades. I've offered you Silver, the one you want, yet you choose to insult me by trying to negotiate. Negotiations are over. If you want to live, leave the girl behind and walk away. If you so much as trim her hair with that medieval sword of yours, I won't hesitate to fire explosive blasts. You now have eight seconds to make your decision."

My jaw hung slack as I watched Elias deliver his threat. I couldn't understand how someone so intimidating could have been kind enough to let us inside. When he pulled away from the speaker, he smiled at us and winked like he was having fun with this.

"Finn, what's the update?" he asked.

"They aren't moving," Finn said.

"Not yet," Elias said. He pressed the button. "Five, four, three..."

"They're moving," Finn said.

Elias grinned. "And the girl?"

"They left her there, on her knees," Finn said. "But what about the army?"

I knew what he was thinking—if we allowed them to live and walk away, wasn't it only a matter of time before they returned? Wouldn't they find another way to come after us? They'd been bold enough to follow us all the way here.

"Don't worry about those idiots," Elias said. "I'm sending out a tank to wipe them out."

"Tank?" someone asked.

"A military tank," Elias said. He formed a large gun with both his hands and started firing invisible bullets, making loud *boom* sounds with his mouth. "They're indestructible machines that can fire explosive blasts."

Most people didn't seem to know what he was talking about. How could they? The war had happened in Grandma's time. The older generation, however, averted their gazes when Elias spoke of the tanks. I couldn't even imagine the traumatic events they must have witnessed as children.

Elias smiled cunningly. "Don't let it scare you, people. It just means you're in good hands here." He smacked his hands together. "Now, how about we get you all showered, fed, and rested?"

CHAPTER 5

A strong wind blew out of metal brackets fastened to the wall.

I'd seen this in Olympus, remembering it so distinctly because it had startled me. Star had explained to me that this was called airflow, and even then, I had a difficult time wrapping my head around it.

"Why not open a window?" I'd asked.

She'd laughed at me and told me to get back to work.

We formed a straight line inside the concrete tunnel, waiting to pass through the doors at the back. With his chin in the air, Elias walked slowly, his brown boots clacking on the hard concrete under our feet. He eyed us carefully as if he were weighing his brother's earlier opinion of us.

Did Elias believe his brother might be right? That we might be dangerous? I expected him to give us a speech about how we would be monitored carefully for the first little while. But he didn't. Instead, he stepped aside, and Finn came forth, leaning on his staff.

Every step looked painful.

Despite his agony, he smiled at us. "I know you're all afraid. But you don't have to be. Right now, all that matters is that you rest and heal. Elias has been kind enough to offer us shelter. I believe it goes without saying that as soon as you are able, you're expected to resume working."

Most people nodded, but a few scowled, seemingly confused.

"Elias and his people will determine your roles," Finn continued. "If you have any concerns, please don't hesitate to come speak with me directly, and I will redirect your concerns to Elias."

"What about the deal?" someone asked.

By deal, he was referring to Finn having agreed to go to war with the Elites. In exchange, Elias would help us defeat the Woodfaces, which he'd done more easily than I could have ever imagined.

Finn paused, weighing his words carefully. I couldn't tell if he regretted his deal, or if he was simply too tired to get into the logistics of it.

"First, we rest," he said. "Then, we can discuss our plan to go after the Elites."

No one said anything. I imagined the last thing anyone wanted to think about right now was going to war.

Nods spread throughout the crowd as people yawned, rubbed their faces, or wiped tears from their cheeks.

"Come," Elias said, breaking the tension. "Let me introduce you to a few new faces."

With an extended hand, he invited us to enter his home.

One by one, people crossed through the door. Holding Sadie's arm around my shoulder, I helped her walk as the line got shorter and shorter. I couldn't believe how quickly people moved through the doorway. How large was the space on the other side? Was there no limit?

The carts, however, didn't move.

When Maz caught me looking at the animals, she winked at me. I wasn't sure what she'd meant by this, but I assumed it was her way of telling me not to worry about her or our livestock—that everything would be fine.

Last, Finn, Reina, Sadie, and I walked through the open door.

I expected the air in here to be as cool as the blowing air from inside the tunnel, but it wasn't. It was neither warm nor cold.

The moment we stepped through, bright white light shined down on us from above. The artificial lighting was similar to that of Olympus, only it was emitted by long tube lights, easily the length of my body. I had expected to walk into a massive room, so I was taken aback to find that our people had formed another line, only this time, in the opposite direction. It was like the two tunnels formed a T.

This tunnel, though not as wide as the entrance we'd come through, extended farther than I could see. The walls were dissimilar, too; rather than the smooth concrete found in the first space, stone ran from the paved floor all the way to the arched ceilings. In front of Sadie and me was a set of large double doors. They looked solid and impenetrable. Although painted black, a bright yellow stripe ran along its bottom edge, catching my eye.

When Elias caught me observing them, he knocked on the hard metal. "This place belonged to the military," he said. "Security was their number one priority."

"Are we going through there?" I asked.

Smiling, he shook his head and aimed his nose down the right side of the tunnel. "No, most of our people stay in the eastern side of the bunker. Anyone who is injured and in need of medical attention will be going that way. Come on."

He led the way, and everyone followed,

filling the space with the sound of footsteps and sharp whispering. Although most people were trying to be quiet, the compilation of it all made it sound like we were being swarmed by thousands of bees.

We stepped into a room so large I couldn't determine which was bigger—this room, or the Village of Ortus. The ceiling was so high I had to crane my neck to look at it. Above, metal pipes and rubber-encased wires ran in various directions. Like the tunnel we'd just exited, the walls were made of rough-looking stone. The floors, however, were solid gray concrete.

Throughout the open space were about a dozen giant pillars that seemed to be holding the structure in place. They were also made of concrete, with black and bright yellow stripes at their bases. I wasn't sure what they were for, but the yellow stripes were apparently a pattern down here.

Maybe it was for decoration.

In the distance stood several dozen vehicles with metal frames and large black tires. Most were square-shaped, but a few were small and looked suited for a single driver.

"This is our parking lot, if you will," Elias said, smirking. He pointed at the back wall, where huge metal doors took up most of the area.

"Does that lead to outside?" Finn asked.

The corners of Elias's mouth curved up again, which I knew meant, *Yes.*

He spun in a circle, showcasing the space. "All vehicles are fully operational. Every week, we allow a few crew members to go out and loot for supplies. I expect some of you will be assisting us with that."

I looked at Sadie, beaming. I'd never ridden in a motorized vehicle before.

She rolled her eyes at me. "Fine, I'll go with you if you volunteer."

Elias kept walking as people whispered and pointed at the vehicles. The space was so large that our footsteps reverberated off the ceiling, sounding like people clapping in the distance.

"This place can be a bit of a maze," Elias shouted, his voice carrying over all of us. "But to simplify it for you, this is the closest you'll come to military equipment. After these doors"—he pointed behind him—"we're entering our civilian area. That means a lounge area, a central social hub, a medical unit, and thousands of sleeping quarters for each of you."

People grew excited as Elias spoke about our new living arrangement.

Jerking his head sideways, he led us through another large metal door with yellow stripes. They opened slowly, as if being controlled electronically, and revealed another tunnel with bright lights, only this one was full of people waiting at the doors. I heard them before I saw them.

"Here is where we're going to split you up into groups," Elias said. "Facilitators will guide you through the bunker, showing you where you can go and what's off-limits."

I stayed close to Sadie as several men and women—facilitators, as Elias had called them—entered the parking area. They smiled at us as they introduced themselves to the people up ahead. Several dozen of them came in, some walking to the back of the crowd, and some remaining at the front.

Using their arms as barriers, they broke us apart into groups of about ten.

While I didn't like the idea of everyone splitting up, it made sense. Managing hundreds of people at once wasn't exactly feasible.

One young man with light brown skin approached Sadie and me. "I'm Alvan," he said, "and I'll be your facilitator today."

He was slender and no taller than me. He had no facial hair, and in its place, a few red pimples told me he was still in his teenage years. His dark eyes glimmered under the overhead lights, and around them were hundreds of thick eyelashes that made me think of Egyptian pictures I'd seen in a few historic books.

He smiled with genuine excitement like he'd been waiting years to be someone's facilitator. Maybe they didn't have a large population here. In Lutum, getting to meet someone new was rare and often exciting.

The large parking space became quieter as more and more people left through various doors.

"Take a good look around. Most Undergrounders don't get to see the vehicles. We'll be exiting through that door." He pointed at a door on the back wall that everyone else had gone through. "This will lead us to the central hub."

"What about Asako?" I blurted out.

Alvan paused, his eyes darting toward Elias. "I'm told she will be sent to our medical center."

Dax took a step forward as if preparing to take a swing at Alvan for no good reason. "What for? Is she injured?"

He shrugged. "I do not have that information. I'm only telling you what was told to me."

He turned around and brought us through the door he'd pointed at. I wasn't surprised to find another vast, long tunnel on the other side. But, unlike the other several spaces I'd walked through, this one had a red floor. Every several yards was a large metal door painted either black or red. I wondered what hid behind them, but I got the feeling we weren't going to be heading through those bright doors anytime soon.

"This door," he said when we ultimately reached the end of the tunnel, "leads us to the living quarters, and from there, the common area. You won't be able to come through this door from the other side." He flashed a plastic-looking badge at us, and when he let it go, it zipped back into place on his belt.

I was stunned by how fast it had flown through the air.

"What is that?" I asked.

"My access card," he said. "You'll get one, too, but you'll be limited to wherever it is you're working."

Another prison.

I pushed the thought away. The only reason I even thought that was because locked doors and special privileges made me think of Olympus. But surely, they'd structured things this way in the bunker for a reason.

I was thankful to be alongside my friends—Sadie, Danika, Dax, and Rose. I wondered how long it would be before we were reunited with Asako. A few other unfamiliar faces followed us closely behind, and I imagined I'd get to know them as time went on.

Farther back, Finn and Reina followed Elias. He was most likely giving them a tour of the entire bunker before sending them to their living quarters. As he walked, he threw his arms in the air, showcasing various doors and explaining what sat behind them.

This wasn't the same Elias I'd seen outside when the tornado was moving in on us.

I supposed now that he was comfortable with us, he'd open up some more.

Alvan brought us through one more tunnel, though it was more of a corridor. This one, unlike the others, was narrow with a low-hanging ceiling. It smelled musty and unclean. Overhead, small circular lights flickered as if on the verge of exploding. They reminded me a bit of fireflies, which then made me think of Grandma.

I'd only ever seen fireflies twice in my life, and when I had, I'd run to Grandma's room, telling her that little flakes of fire were floating outside my bedroom window. She'd wrapped her arms around me and led me back to my room, kissing the top of my head.

"They're just bugs, sweetheart," she told me at the time. "And you know what else?" She pointed outside my window as countless little lights flickered near a raspberry bush. "When they flash like that, it's for love."

She pulled me in then and shook me

playfully. "And when you see them, be thankful they're small like that. Some species can be the size of your palm."

My eyes had bulged at the thought of a huge insect landing in my room.

She'd given me one more kiss before leaving me alone, mesmerized as I watched these little insects talk to one another.

"Why is it doing that?" I asked Alvan, pointing above.

"Bulb needs to be changed," he said. "We're running low."

I looked at Sadie.

"A light bulb," she said.

I nodded as if I understood how it worked and kept moving.

When Alvan reached the end of the narrow corridor, he rested his palm on the silver handle and looked back at us with his big, black-outlined eyes. "This leads to Hallway C. We have a total of eight, and each one contains two hundred private rooms."

Two hundred?

How could a single hallway contain two hundred rooms?

"Each one ties back to the central hub." Then, he smiled, and there was a cute, childish way about him. "Think of this place like a giant spider. We're about to walk into one of its legs."

With that, he opened the door, and the

sound of a few voices rang out nearby. They were familiar. I craned my neck to look past his shoulder, and at the same time, Lyson and Lyla looked back at me. Lyson smiled, while his sister didn't. This wasn't a surprise. Ever since I'd met her, I got the feeling she didn't like me.

"Silver!" Lyson called out. He jogged toward me, his footsteps echoing throughout the hallway.

I blinked hard, trying to see the end of the hallway behind Lyson, but I couldn't. Alvan hadn't been exaggerating. There were hundreds of doors in here.

When he caught up with us, his chest inflated as he fought to catch his breath. "Can you believe this place? I mean, look at all these rooms!"

He pointed at the door nearest to me, where silver, metallic letters read, H1.

The farther up I looked, the letters seemed to be climbing.

H2, H3, H4.

The doors ran along both sides of the walls. They, too, were made of metal. Everything down here seemed made of either metal or concrete. It made the whole place feel solid and indestructible.

"I'm in H96," Lyson said. "Where are you?"

I looked at Alvan, who smiled. "Facilitators were instructed to fill vacant rooms first," he said.

"Lyson!" Lyla called out. "Get over here."

"Gotta go," Lyson said. "I'll catch you later, okay?"

He ran off to meet up with his sister and the rest of their group. One by one, they disappeared into individual rooms. When Lyson's turn came up, he disappeared only for a second, then popped his head out of his room and opened his mouth as wide as he could, which was his way of showing how amazed he was at the interior.

It was funny, and despite how tired and how much pain I was in, it made me smile.

Without a word, Alvan brought us to where the other group had been only moments ago.

"These are vacant." He started with H100 and scanned his badge in front of a little flickering panel on the wall. The door slid open, making a grating sound, and disappeared entirely. "Go ahead and choose. They're all the same inside."

He moved on to the other doors, opening them one at a time.

I wasn't sure why, but I darted to room 101 the moment he opened it. There was something about that number that I loved. Maybe it had something to do with Grandma telling me the story of the 101 Dalmatians.

Before entering, I turned around to look at

Sadie, hoping she'd choose the room next to mine—H103.

Unfortunately, someone else was already walking to it—a bulky guy with a scruffy face and blood all over his forest green shirt. He walked briskly with his arm in a sling, and although I didn't recognize him, it was obvious by the way he carried himself that he was a Champion.

"Hudson, move it," Sadie said.

Hudson, the man with the sling, stood at the entrance of H103 and cocked a brow at her. "What do you mean, move—"

"That's my room," she said.

He huffed at her. "I don't see your name on it."

"Not yet," she said. "But you will if you don't move, and I'll use your blood to write it."

He glared at her, probably trying to decide whether the room was worth the trouble. After an intense standoff, he grumbled something and moved on to room H105.

Sadie grinned at me like nothing had happened and disappeared into her room.

"Get comfortable," Alvan said. "Rest up. And if you'd like to join us, Elias is hosting a celebration this evening to welcome all of you. See that door?" He aimed a finger at the very end of the hallway. It was nearly impossible to see the door from here, but I assumed it was positioned on the back wall. "When you're ready, go through that door. The celebration starts at five."

I blinked hard, hoping I'd remember the details.

"And in case you're wondering, there's a button, right here—" Alvan moved toward my room, making me step back into it. He leaned inside and reached for a red button on the wall, but didn't press it. "That controls your door. And don't worry, there are safety features in place. It won't close if someone is standing in the way."

I was thankful he'd mentioned that. All I could envision was getting squished by the huge metal door.

"To control it from the outside," he continued, "you'll need your access badges. We'll take care of that later. For now, leave your doors open when you leave."

He turned around, prepared to walk away. "Oh, I almost forgot. Showers are limited to five minutes to conserve water. We use an on-demand hot water system, so the water should always be hot, but like I said—five minutes. After that, it will automatically shut off. You have everything you need in there." He pointed inside at what looked like a bathroom. "Soap, shampoo, towels. When you're done with your towels, place them in the bathroom delivery slot. You'll recognize it when you see it. Someone will take it and replace it with a fresh towel."

Finished with the tour, he made his way down the hallway and disappeared.

I turned to Sadie, wanting to say something along the lines of, *Wow, can you believe this place?* but she was already gone.

So I pressed the red button, in total awe as the heavy metal door slid shut. The moment it closed, all sound disappeared.

Slowly, I turned around, admiring the sight before me. How was this even possible? After what I'd seen of the bunker, I expected more concrete, and maybe a flimsy metal-framed bed—not that I would have minded it at all. I was thankful for anything I received. But surprisingly, the floors were covered in sparkling red and white tiles, as were half the walls. The remaining upper half of the walls was matte black, and although the style wasn't something I'd ever seen or pictured before, it mesmerized me. Next to the entrance was a bathroom. But unlike the bathroom the Breeders and I had shared in Olympus—a dirty yellow room with cracked tiles—this one was so clean and sparkly I had to keep reminding myself it was a bathroom.

Entering the bathroom, I admired the decor. Over the toilet sat a little black shelf with some sort of bamboo plant, its roots hidden within rounded black and white rocks. Next to the toilet was a glass-door shower, and on the other side of the bathroom, a beautiful white-stone sink with a shiny metal faucet.

A few months ago, this room would have looked like the inside of an alien spaceship to me.

In awe, I ventured through the rest of my new room. It was only big enough to fit a bed and a night table, but that was all I needed. The bedsheets—also a red, black, and white design—made me want to climb in and sleep for a week.

But I was filthy, and I needed to shower.

So I returned to the bathroom, undressed, and entered the shower. As hot water cleansed my face and dripped over my eyes, I inhaled a deep breath, water tickling my lips and splashing into my mouth. When I opened my eyes again, the shower's white base had filled with a pink liquid—blood mixed with water.

I scrubbed and scrubbed until the water ran clear.

CHAPTER 6

"Did any of you sleep?" Sadie asked, stepping out into the narrow hallway.

Dax shook her head, as did Danika and Rose.

"No," I admitted. "You?"

She gave me a tired look that told me she hadn't slept, either, and we made our way toward the back door Alvan had pointed to earlier. As much as I'd wanted to sleep beforehand, I couldn't. In my mind, all I kept replaying was the prior day's attack—all of our people dying, the screams, the fire, the sound of bones crushing.

It was like a picture book constantly flashing in my mind, with pages flipping on their own.

The crowd thickened in the hallway as more of our people came out, including Lyson and Lyla.

When we finally got to the end of the

hallway, no one reached for the door handle. Instead, they turned to me, waiting.

"Do the honors," Sadie said.

I wasn't even sure what she meant, but I got the feeling the others were letting me go through first. Turning the knob, I pushed through.

To my surprise, the large room was mostly empty, aside from a few people sitting in red fabric chairs. The second I opened the door, Alvan jolted out of one of the chairs, his scrawny legs looking too long for his body. He beamed at us, clasped his hands in front of his flat, almost nonexistent belly, and bowed politely. "Ah, so glad you decided to join the celebration."

The room was shaped like a giant decagon, with eight regular-sized doors on either side and two larger doors at the front and back. Overhead, stunning chandeliers filled the room with an orange glow. It didn't match the rest of the bare bunker, but I assumed they'd done it this way on purpose.

The floor—large black and white tiles—spread throughout the entire space, disappearing under chairs, tables, and metallic benches. What caught my attention most of all were the walls; they were painted blue and green, almost as if to give off the impression that we were either outside or underwater.

Either way, it was fascinating, and serene.

"This is the common hub," Alvan said. "People meet here to spend time together—to socialize and to relax, or to wait for friends. But we have much more." He jerked his chin at the very back door. "This way."

A few strangers watched us curiously as we followed Alvan, likely wondering who we were. No one spoke to us, though, and I wondered if they were upset at the idea of having newcomers, or excited to officially meet us.

Where he led us next made my jaw drop.

Although the space was open and massive much like the parking lot, it was bare. Dark brown wood ran up the walls and across the high ceiling in an arch. Silver-rimmed chandeliers hung from the wooden beams, lighting up the space with a natural light much unlike the white lights from earlier.

Countless wooden tables and chairs ran along each wall. A peculiar counter, like nothing I'd seen before, was in the back. Behind it, bottles of all different shapes and sizes shimmered underneath dangling yellow lights. Inside were liquids of various colors, but I had no idea what they were.

Most of the tables were occupied by groups of people I didn't recognize. Unlike Ortus and Lutum, these people wore all kinds of strange clothes. Some were colorful—mostly women's tops—while many wore faded blue pants. Where had the clothes come from? The outside world?

On the right wall were all the strangers, while on the left, our people. And at the very front table, near the countless bottles of liquid, were Finn, Reina, Maz, and a few other heads of Ortus.

I wondered if Elias had intentionally separated us all, or if no one had gotten around to introducing themselves yet.

"This way," Alvan said, bringing us to an empty table.

We sat down, and I felt awkward as countless eyes watched our every movement. It felt hostile, for the most part. Others, however, seemed excited, almost like they were on the verge of jolting upright and running across the room to come shake our hands.

Then, across from me, I recognized someone.

Elias's brother, Jared.

He looked the most vicious of all of them. He sat with a rounded back, his stubbled chin hovering over a large, frosted glass containing some honey-colored liquid. It was mostly full, yet he didn't drink it.

He sat there, tapping his fingers against the cool-looking glass, watching us.

Unlike most other citizens in the room, he still wore that strange tactical-type uniform. It was black, with shoulder pads, elbow pads, knee pads, and a chest plate. I couldn't tell what it was made out of, but it looked sturdy enough to block an arrow. It reminded me a bit of the Defenders, only far less advanced and less durable.

His boots were filthy, and their tips were covered in a layer of dirt. Maybe he'd just come from outside, having gone out looking for supplies.

Around him sat other men and women wearing the same outfits. They, too, looked dirty, like they hadn't taken the time to shower after their travels and had instead come straight to the ceremony.

Where had they gone? Had Jared been sent out to kill the Woodfaces?

"Don't mind him," Sadie said, watching me. "He looks like a miserable bastard."

"I think he's just cautious," I said. "Wouldn't you be? If a bunch of strangers entered your home?"

She gave me a blank stare that told me she agreed with me, but didn't care to admit it.

The room became quiet when one last group came through the back door.

I smiled at them, even though I didn't know them. Three children followed their mother closely, and the second they sat down, Danika smiled big at them. She must have worked with the children in Ortus's daycare.

"Thank you for coming," Elias shouted.

I didn't recognize him at first without his hat. Instead, his curly black locks were fastened in a small bun at the back of his head. It made him look clean and professional, not like the same Elias who had ordered his people to wipe out an entire army.

He stepped forward, revealing slick black pants and a blue button-up top, which also made him look much more approachable than earlier.

His loud, overpowering voice spread through the space with ease.

"I'm certain many of you are confused as to why I brought you here." With a puffed chest, he opened his palm at his people. "But I'm thinking you already figured it out."

He smirked, and a few people laughed. It became obvious that Elias was liked by his people—or at least *most* of his people—and that they thought him funny.

"We have some new faces that will be joining our colony," he said. Before anyone could say anything, he stuck out a flat palm. "Now, before you bombard me with questions, let me make a few things perfectly clear. These people are *not* our enemies. We share a

64

common goal, and that's our hatred for the Elites."

Several people on the other side nodded excitedly like they were surprised to hear this.

"And some of you might be concerned about our rations, but I assure you, these fine folks will help us double our production and will certainly manage to feed themselves."

He turned to Finn, who gave him a courteous nod.

"So, tonight is about meeting new faces and celebrating," he said.

Behind him, a woman with a high ponytail, light brown skin, and a charming smile moved closer. She grabbed a bottle, causing a clanging sound to resonate throughout the room, and poured some of its contents into a short, square-shaped glass. She slid it across the countertop, right behind Elias.

He thanked her and grabbed the glass, then raised it before bringing it back down and taking a sip out of it.

"Food will be served shortly," he said. "Anyone over the age of twenty-one is welcome to indulge in a drink or two," he continued, licking his lips. "Come see Mia at the bar. Everyone else, we have water, juice, milk—your pick."

Twenty-one? Why was there an age restriction for a beverage?

Sadie laughed at my contorted face. "It's alcohol."

My face didn't change.

"It alters your state. Relaxes you. Not that I'd know, I've never had any. But I've watched Finn and Reina get *buzzed* a few times. That's what they called it. Kind of disturbing, if you ask me. Reina laughs a lot when she's buzzed. Finn gets loud."

I wanted to say something like, "Good thing you haven't had any. You'd probably rip your smiling muscles," but kept the comment to myself. As funny as I found it, I got the feeling she wouldn't appreciate my humor.

Most adults made their way to the back and formed a line to get a glass of *alcohol*. Kids were brought orange or apple juice, while my friends and I waited for the lines to cool down before going to get our drinks.

Dax was the first to jolt upright. She'd been staring at Mia—the woman behind the bar—since Elias had introduced her. When she ran off to the bar, Danika rolled her eyes. "She's like a cat on a mouse, that one."

We followed, grabbing our drinks as Dax chatted up a storm with Mia, then returned to our table. Slowly—and as more people drank their alcohol—the two sides began to mix. People smiled at each other, shook hands, and introduced themselves, making connections. I met a few people who seemed surprised to learn that me and my friends—aside from Sadie—had come from Lutum.

It caused such an ordeal that a little crowd formed around our table.

When the food came, everyone returned to their tables. It was served by the same people who had brought us loaves of bread when we'd first entered the bunker. Had these people volunteered to serve others? I hoped so. The last thing I wanted was to find myself in another place where people were forced to do things against their will.

But they looked happy as they headed for various tables, pushing tall wooden carts with rubber wheels. On each cart were plates full of steaming vegetables, mashed potatoes, and a side of meat.

The boy who served us—a red-haired boy with freckles across his nose—beamed as he placed each plate down in front of us. "This is a real treat," he said. "We don't often eat red meat, so consider yourselves lucky."

I thought of our cows, and I couldn't help but wonder where this meat had come from. Had they slaughtered one of ours? I hoped not. I didn't like the idea of slaughtering any animal, but I wasn't one to say no to food when it was given to me.

Some people chatted as we ate, while

others remained quiet, savoring every bite. My eyelids fluttered as I ate, sinking my teeth into the fire-roasted and salted carrots. Halfway through my meal, the music came on.

It started with a loud boom sound that made me flinch, and was then followed by upbeat music that seemed to travel into our tables and up my fingertips.

Then, the yellow overhead lights dimmed and colorful lights filled the room. One by one, people moved to the open space at the center of the room and started dancing. It made me uncomfortable. The only time I'd seen anyone dance—aside from Grandma—was during Penelope's Celebration of Life, when Arahm had made a fire and musicians had hit their drums, chanting.

As I finished my meal, I closed my eyes, appreciating every beat the song had to offer.

There was something so magical about music.

"Hey, Silver, come join us," Lyson said, his white-blond hair appearing out of nowhere.

He grinned from ear to ear, took a sip of his juice, then placed it down on our table. It made a slight splash, and Sadie grimaced.

"Come on. You have to try it. This music is unreal." He offered me a hand.

I hesitated, despite everyone around me laughing and dancing to the beat of the song.

Sadie nudged me. "Just go," she shouted over the music. "Have fun."

Blue and green lights flickered, and I blinked hard.

"You get used to the lights!" Lyson shouted. "Come on!"

He barely gave me time to reach for him. Extending his long arm, he grabbed my wrist and pulled me into the moving crowd. Heat radiated from everyone's bodies as the room shook—or at least, it felt like it was shaking.

Lyson wasn't shy about dancing, either.

He swept his hips from side to side. He looked *goofy*, as Grandma would say, and it made me laugh. It was apparent he didn't know what he was doing, but he didn't seem to care. Next, he balled his fists and started pumping them in the air, matching the song's beat. A few other people did the same, and I wondered if he'd learned it from them.

Every few seconds, he paused, watched someone else dance, then tried to mimic their movements.

"Come on!" he shouted again. He grabbed me by the shoulders and started swaying them from side to side.

I felt so uncomfortable. What if people were watching? What if Sadie was watching? I peeked through the crowd to look at her, but the second we made eye contact, she turned away and started up a conversation with Danika.

"Just let loose!"

Let loose? What did that even mean?

He pointed at his leg and started moving it to the music. "Now you, go!" He pointed at my leg.

I did the same thing, tapping my heel against the floor every time the drums hit. It felt oddly... fun. Next, I moved my head from side to side, matching the song's rhythm.

"That's it! That's it!" He spun in a circle and started hopping up and down, punching the air.

I burst out laughing as his hair flopped on his head with every jump.

But after his third jump, he landed funny. It wasn't until the person next to him winced and pulled away that I realized he'd landed on their foot. Before having the time to apologize to the stranger, Lyson stumbled toward me, his wide, panicked eyes warning me that he'd lost his balance.

I didn't have time to move, either.

He crashed into me, propelling me backward. The blow was so hard I couldn't stop myself from falling with him pressed into me. I anticipated falling into someone behind me and maybe causing a few people to tumble over, but what happened next was even worse.

A sharp pain exploded in my head as we fell into a wooden table, sending chairs, plates, and drinks all over the place. It made a loud crashing sound—loud enough for people to turn to us, despite the booming music. Cold liquid spilled on the floor, pooling around my elbow. Next to my face were large, dirty boots that seemed all too familiar.

They pulled away from me and were immediately followed by the sound of a chair screeching.

The man stood up, cursing, and reached for Lyson who had fallen next to me after landing on the table. He grabbed him by his collar, ripping part of his shirt, and raised him onto his feet.

Grabbing my head, I stood up to find Jared face-to-face with Lyson, spewing insults almost directly into his mouth. He bared his teeth like a wild animal and pulled him in so close that their noses touched. Lyson looked terrified. He kept shouting about how sorry he was, and how it had been an accident. But Jared didn't seem to care. His muscles bulged through his black uniform as he shook Lyson.

I was surprised that the rest of his shirt didn't rip off.

Why was Jared lashing out at him? It was an accident.

I clenched my fists, prepared to throw

myself at Jared, when out of nowhere, he flew sideways, losing his grip on Lyson and falling into a pile of chairs. I blinked hard, trying to understand what had happened.

Sadie stood there, scowling at Jared with a hunched posture as if she were preparing to fight to the death if necessary.

"You okay?" she yelled my way.

I was too stunned to say anything.

When Jared got back up, he gave Sadie a death stare that told me he wanted her blood.

He moved toward her, and at the same time, I reached for one of the fallen wooden chairs. With all of my strength, I swung sideways, preparing for the chair to break into bits on his back.

But to my surprise, someone grabbed the chair, stopping me midattack.

One of Jared's followers.

Being unable to finish the blow made me feel awful.

The large man yanked the chair out of my grip, and Jared watched, probably in disbelief that I'd tried to hit him with it in the first place.

He pulled his upper lip over his teeth, likely growling, though it was impossible to hear with the loud music.

At once, the music cut out and the regular yellow lights came back on.

Gasps filled the space as people began to

realize what was happening. Then, the crowd split, and through the opening gap came Elias and Finn.

"What is the meaning of this?" Elias growled.

Jared seethed. "These two halfwits crashed into me and my—"

"They're kids, for God's sake!" Elias shouted. "Grow up, brother, would you?"

Jared's hateful eyes scanned our audience. I could sense his anger from where I stood. It was no longer directed at us, but rather, at his brother. After all, Elias had humiliated him in front of his followers.

I was taken aback when a sly smile tugged at his lips. Why was he smiling like that? Only seconds ago, he'd looked like his head might explode. Yet that smile told me he was preparing to do something awful.

"So you defend these strangers over your own family!" Jared shouted, purposely trying to make his voice heard by everyone.

"This isn't about taking sides," Elias said.

"Isn't it?" his brother snarled. "You cut me off before I could even explain myself. You don't care about your people. You want fresh bodies. You want more *workers* to produce for you. That's what this is all about. Isn't it, *King* Elias?

"That's absurd!" Elias said. His shoulders

expanded as he took a step toward Jared. "These people have done nothing wrong. If you want to be close-minded and refuse entry to innocent souls, then you're no better than the Elites. You're selfish, and you want to keep everything—"

"I will not stand here while you berate me!" Jared shouted. His voice came out deep, like a roar, making me feel small.

Others must have sensed his fury, too. No one spoke; everyone stood silently, watching.

"Your people deserve better than what you give them," Jared said, calming his tone. "They deserve to feel safe, and bringing in hundreds of people who will eat up our rations within a few days is not safety!"

Elias parted his lips, on the verge of defending himself, when Jared clenched his jaw and said, "Come on, let's go." He turned around, his dozen or so followers sticking close behind.

After that, the celebration ended.

CHAPTER 7

As we emerged from the underground bunker, the sun felt like Grandma's kiss on my cheek.

Although blinding, I was thankful to have it beaming down on my face.

Today was the day we were to be assigned a role.

"Most people prefer to work outside," Elias said. "Everyone has access to the courtyard." He extended his arms on either side of him to showcase their outdoor sanctuary.

Stone walls, reaching several yards toward the sky, surrounded us. In front of them, flower beds boasted of vibrant yellows, pinks, and greens. On the southern wall were giant hinges and a straight crease, which told me the walls opened up. But the moss and vines growing over them also told me the gates were rarely opened.

Was that how Maz moved all the livestock

in here? Chickens clucked in the distance as an older gentleman helped rehome them into a smaller chicken coop in the corner of the courtyard. It looked dark inside, and he brought them in one by one before closing the door and leaving them there.

Although they'd been secluded, other black chickens with bright red combs roamed about freely. They weren't ours—ours were white and brown—and I wondered if they'd soon be introduced.

Next to the coop was a stable much larger than the one we'd had in Ortus, though half of its structure was crumbled and all of its horses remained outside, tied to posts with rope. I imagined they didn't ride them as often as we did. Why would they? They had an entire lot full of functioning vehicles.

And what had happened to their stable? A few other nearby structures also looked to be in bad shape. Some were missing roofs, while others had collapsed entirely.

Smiling, Elias squinted as the morning sunrays hit him in the face. "The courtyard is usually much nicer," he admitted. "The tornado hit us hard." He paused, staring off at the damaged wooden structures. "Now, I have a matter to attend to, but I trust your facilitators will explain to you what happens next."

He tipped his hat at us and went back

through the door we'd exited from.

Alvan appeared at our sides as if by magic, then smacked his hands together. "Now," he said, "it's time for orientation."

Orientation?

Dozens of facilitators led their groups to the western wall, where plastic tables—much like the ones in Olympus's pillars—had been stationed side by side. Behind them, people of different heights, genders, and colors stood proudly in front of hand-drawn posters that hung at the front of each table.

Clothing

Building

Agriculture

Livestock

Equipment

Machinery

Cleaning

Cooking

Where was the Champions list? Fighters? Protectors? Why weren't any of those an option? I turned to Finn, who was too preoccupied staring at the posters to notice me looking. Reina, on the other hand, caught my stare. She leaned into Finn and whispered something.

Finn shook his head as if saying, *Not right now,* and Reina kept walking.

It wasn't long before whispers broke out

across the courtyard.

"I thought we were going to fight the Elites," Dax said. "How are we supposed to do that if we can't even train?"

She wasn't alone in thinking that way. Countless other Champions scowled at the tables, bickering back and forth. The arguing grew so loud that the facilitators exchanged confused glances.

"What about fighting?" someone shouted as we drew in nearer.

The volunteers behind the tables looked at each other, too, not knowing how to answer. Most of them forced a polite smile, despite their obvious frustration.

Then, from across the field came a familiar face—Sofia.

She jogged toward us in her black, shoulder-padded military uniform. On her belt was a gun, though I doubted she had ever used it in the courtyard. With no one able to enter, how was anyone in danger?

The closest danger these people had probably ever come to was the tornado.

"What's going on?" Sofia asked.

She stood tall, her figure casting a shadow across Sadie's forehead. With two hands on her weapons belt, she turned to Finn for clarification.

"I believe my people are wondering why

there's no option to join your group of fighters," he said plainly.

"We're following Elias's orders," Sofia said. "We need hands to help rebuild what's been damaged, and we need more food, supplies, and materials if we all want to live comfortably here."

Finn nodded. "Understood."

"But—" someone tried.

Finn raised a solid fist and they went quiet.

"We're guests here," Finn said. "If these are Elias's orders, then we follow them."

A few Champions grumbled, but no one argued.

"Now," Finn said, "I suggest you all split up evenly among the different roles. Otherwise, some of you will have to be reassigned. I'd much rather you choose for yourself."

People turned their backs and rushed to various tables. Almost everyone avoided the Cleaning and Cooking tables, except for Arahm and his children, who darted straight for the Cooking table. A few other middle-aged men and women lined up in front of the Cleaning table, but they were in the minority.

I walked up to Agriculture, since it was what I knew best.

"Why don't you try something new?" Sadie said, lining up at the table next to me.

I leaned forward to read the sign: *Building.*

I must have twisted my face. She laughed, and said, "You got a problem with my choice?"

"Why would you want to build stuff?" I asked.

She gave me a flat-lidded look like I was an idiot. "I need to use my hands. I need to move."

Most other Builders were men, and only a few were women. Dax had lined up behind Machinery, Danika behind Clothing, and Rose behind Cooking, which surprised me the most.

She smiled at me, her dark cheeks forming little balloons under her eyes. Arahm seemed excited to have a young fresh face willing to learn how to cook. He wrapped his arm around her, making her eyes bulge out at me, and shook her hard. "Great to have you on the team!" he said.

I scanned the crowd, watching lines form in front of the various tables, when I caught Lyson and Lyla's bright heads. They stood with the Livestock line. I remembered Lyson telling me he worked in the library in Ortus. Maybe before that, he'd worked with the animals.

One by one, the lines shortened as people gave their names to the volunteers behind the tables. When it was my turn, the girl asked me, "Room number?"

"H101," I said.

"Name?"

"Silver," I said. "Blackwood."

"Qualifications or reason for your choice?" she asked.

"Um, I used to do this," I said.

She glanced up at me from her sheet of paper.

"In Lutum," I clarified. "I was a Producer in Division 9, the agriculture division."

Her eyes popped. "Lutum?" Sounding a bit terrified, she scribbled my name, handed me a shiny card, and swept her hand at me as if to say, *Go on, all good. Now get out of here.*

"What's this?" I asked, grabbing the little piece of plastic. At its end was a circular gadget much like the one Alvan had attached to his belt. When I pulled on the card, a little black rope zipped out of it.

"Your access card," she said. "It gives you courtyard privileges, among a few other common room areas. It'll also give you access to your room from the outside."

She stared at me, waiting for me to leave.

I was accustomed to people growing uncomfortable at the sound of Lutum, but I hadn't expected someone to be afraid of *me*, as if I somehow carried an infectious disease.

I followed the others from my table toward dozens upon dozens of garden beds at the center of the courtyard. Unlike what we'd had in Lutum, these were raised beds constructed of finely sanded cedarwood shaped into long rectangles.

"Hi there," someone said.

Next to me was a short, pudgy woman with a few wrinkles around her eyes, red and gray hair, and lips that looked like they'd never smiled before. She watched me with cold eyes, analyzing every inch of me. "Name?"

"Silver," I said.

She gave me a green-handled spade, hitting me hard in the chest with it. It almost fell, but I somehow caught it at my waist.

"That bed." She pointed at the farthest bed. "Take out the weeds."

I nodded, prepared to obey, when I realized I didn't even know this woman's name. If we were going to be working with each other every day, I didn't want us to be enemies.

"Wh-what's your name?" I asked.

She gave me a venomous look that made me want to swallow my words and turn around.

We stared at each other for a few seconds, and when I realized she wasn't going to give me her name, I made my way over to the garden bed full of weeds. Many others from Ortus sat on the edges, plucking out weeds.

One young man, in particular, whistled a tune as he reached into the vegetable plants and tore out ugly weeds. When he saw me approach, he smiled sweetly at me. "Welcome to Agriculture!"

I knew this man.

Elliot—the man who had kept Sadie and me safe behind the mountain after the Woodfaces attacked for the first time.

He must have recognized me, too.

"Wait, aren't you Silver?" he said. "I remember you, darling."

He still wore his leather vest and swayed his hips as he moved. "Where's Sadie? I haven't seen her since—"

"Since we were attacked," I said.

I was surprised to see him here.

"You look surprised to see me," he said as if reading my mind. He planted a hand on his right hip and shifted his weight onto one leg. "We were bringing back your horses after the Woodfaces attacked the main entrance." His black-outlined eyes dropped to my feet. "You guys left right in time."

"What do you mean?" I asked.

As Elliot and I spoke, countless heads turned our way, wanting in on the conversation.

"I heard Finn collapsed the tunnel," he said. "On a horse, or something."

"Yeah, he did," I said.

Elliot's eyes glazed over as he no doubt imagined what that moment must have been like. He smiled at the fantasy and sighed. "So heroic.”

I clicked my fingers in front of his face to get him to snap out of it, when out of nowhere, Sadie came bolting toward him and threw her arms around his neck. He was so frail that he almost fell back.

She winced on impact and pulled away, clutching at the wound on her abdomen.

“Where the hell have you been, asshole?” She coughed, wincing some more. “I’ve been looking for you.”

“I was trying to keep my little brother calm,” he said. “I meant to come see you, but every time I tried to get up, he’d cry.”

Sadie smiled knowingly. “It’s okay. I’m glad you’re alive.”

A tiny smile tugged at his lips and he pointed at the blood seeping through her shirt. “Me too, but you don’t look so good.”

She reached for the blood, pulling red fingers up to eye level. “Damn it.”

“You should go see your facilitator, love,” he said. “There’s a medical unit in the bunker. I was there overnight with my brother. He’s been having so much anxiety that they had to sedate him.”

Sadie’s brow slanted. “I’m sorry to hear that.”

Elliot flicked a wrist. “Don’t be. It is what it is. He’ll be okay. You know how it is. Trauma takes time to heal."

I wasn't sure who Elliot's brother was, but by the way he spoke of him, I imagined he was only a child. I felt sorry for him. How much of the war had he witnessed? Had he been injured? Burned? Had he seen people around him die? Probably.

"How'd you even get here?" Sadie asked.

"Like I was telling your friend, here," he continued, "we were bringing your horses back. That's when we saw the army and the tunnel. You should've seen it, Sadie. Hundreds of them." His outlined eyes went big as he swung his arms in every direction, as if trying to paint an invisible image for us. "We had to leave the horses behind, but we made it back to the village in boats."

He looked sad about it, and I felt awful at the thought of our horses being left alone near Death Valley. Would they run off and live freely? Or, would they be captured and used by others?

"Go on, get yourself looked at," Elliot said, eyeballing Sadie's bloodstained shirt.

She rolled her eyes and smiled. "I think last night's brawl with Jared loosened my stitches."

"Jared? Elias's brother?" Elliot asked, his mouth dropping into a huge smile. "You feisty little bitch."

Sadie grabbed him by the head and kissed

his forehead. "Catch you later."

She turned around and found Alvan, who then guided her to the bunker's entrance. From there, other people led her inside and she disappeared.

"Better get to work, chica," Elliot said. "Viv doesn't look too happy."

"Viv?" I asked.

He twirled his spade at the red-and-gray-haired woman who hadn't given me her name.

"Vivian," he said. "She runs the garden beds. Word has it she's a real hoot."

Hoot. I'd never heard this before, but I got the feeling Elliot was being sarcastic. I liked how he spoke so informally, the way Grandma used to.

The woman glowered at us from underneath a huge white, floral hat she must have just put on. When she caught me watching her, she patted dirt off her garden gloves, huffed, bent down, and dug inside of a bush.

CHAPTER 8

Our groups met in the same room we'd danced in the night before, only this time, the tension was even higher. The people of Ortus remained separate from the Undergrounders, talking only among themselves.

What had happened? Was this because of Jared? I couldn't imagine what else was causing it. It wasn't like we'd attacked the people—our conflict had been with Jared only. Yet, crowds bickered and glossy eyes narrowed on us.

It felt hostile, reminding me of Lutum.

"What's their problem?" I asked.

Sadie wasn't there to answer me. Hopefully, it wouldn't take too long for her to receive new stitches.

"I don't think they're happy about us wanting to fight," Dax said. "A lot of Champions were complaining about it today. About how we shouldn't be wasting time plucking weeds or cleaning clothes."

"Well, it's true," Hudson said.

With Sadie gone, he dared to speak. Leaning forward, he pressed his bulky chest against the edge of the table and eyed the Undergrounders, his blond eyebrows remaining flat on his forehead. "The whole point of the deal Finn made was to come together to fight the Elites. We can't exactly do that if we stop training. We'll become deconditioned."

"We also need to sustain ourselves," I said, matter-of-factly.

I didn't like the idea of no longer training, either, but Elias was right to make us work before we prepared to fight. Many of us still needed time to heal, both physically and emotionally.

Hudson rolled his eyes at me and leaned back in his chair, holding on to his sling. "If I can help repair a stable with one arm, I can keep training. We have more than enough people who can do the other boring stuff. Let Champions be Champions."

"This is why they're upset," Danika cut in. "Hundreds of us show up, and a third of our people want to throw weapons around instead of being part of sustaining this society."

Hudson didn't say anything. Instead, he kept glaring at the Undergrounders as if trying to intimidate them. It was annoying, and Danika was right—this was the exact kind of behavior that could keep us divided.

That's when I realized Sadie wasn't the only one missing from the table. "Where's Dax?"

Rose shrugged, as did everyone else around the table.

As though she wanted to be found, her loud, boisterous laugh filled the entire room. She sat on the other side, among the Undergrounders. Specifically, she sat next to Mia—the girl from behind the bar. They leaned into each other, whispering things and laughing every few seconds.

Smiling at the ceiling, Danika shook her head.

"At least some people are getting along," I said.

We ate supper mostly in silence until Alvan returned us to our rooms. It wasn't until the third day that he stopped guiding us everywhere. He stuck around, in case we had any questions—such as where we went to do our laundry, or where we could pick up additional supplies like soap if we ran out. He was kind and helpful.

As the days went on, the Champions seemed to become more complacent. It was for the best. Pouting or complaining wouldn't get them what they wanted, and every time someone commented in the courtyard, I reminded them of where we were and how if it weren't for Elias and his people, we'd all be dead. The least we could do was respect Elias's demands.

This worked, for the most part.

Dax and Sadie played their parts, too, but they weren't as friendly about it. Sadie went around telling people to shut up, and Dax threatened to punch guys in the face if they didn't quit their whining. Every time Dax threatened someone, though, she'd shoot a glance in Mia's general direction, like she was trying to impress her.

It was cute.

In my area, I rarely had to speak up. Elliot did most of the talking for me.

"We've been doing this for days," said one female Champion. Without gloves, she stretched her long arms into a garden bed and pulled out a handful of green beans. Tossing them into a wicker basket, she grimaced. "Why isn't Finn saying anything? I mean, look"—she threw her chin out toward the stables and a few other structures that were now repaired—"everything's back up. We don't belong here. We should be—"

"Oh, quit your lip flappin', girl," Elliot said. "No one wants to hear it."

A few men around him hesitated. They

enjoyed hearing people complain about our circumstances, but they didn't want to get on Elliot's bad side.

"I've been listening to you bitch like a banshee for the last two days," he went on. "You're acting like a damn slave. Is that how you feel? Like a slave?" His dark-outlined eyes appeared above a bush, and he glared at her so intensely that she retreated behind hers. When she didn't reappear, he turned to me. "Silver, do you feel like a slave, here?"

I thought of our evening suppers, the fresh air, our private rooms, our showers, and found myself thankful for everything I had. In a sense, it all reminded me of Lutum, only because I was once again working in a garden and a few armed people stood nearby. But I knew they weren't here to enforce our work requirements. Every time I glanced over at Sofia, she'd smile at me without reaching for a weapon. Sometimes, I looked at her several times a day, only to remind myself that she wasn't a Defender.

I hadn't gone back in time.

I was safe now.

Her smile reassured me of that.

"This isn't Lutum," I said, gritting my teeth. While there were similarities, the two places were nothing alike, and the last thing I needed was to be verbally reminded of Lutum.

"Listen to the girl," Elliot said. "If you want to see what it feels like to be a real slave, go on, walk your pretty little booty to Lutum and ask them to let you in."

I wasn't sure why Elliot was still going on about this. The girl was nowhere to be seen. She likely felt embarrassed for having been called out for nonstop complaining.

"Give the girl a break," said someone else. The man was middle-aged with severe sun damage across his cheeks. He didn't look to be a Champion. He'd likely been a gardener in Ortus, too. "She only wants to do what she knows best."

"And she will," Elliot said. This time, he stood up, dropped his spade, and grabbed his hips. He stared at everyone as if trying to injure them with his eyes. "But complaining isn't doing us any favors! All you're doing is pissing off the fine folks who live here."

One woman smiled up at him, and he winked at her. I didn't recognize her, and by the way she was dressed, it was obvious she was an Undergrounder.

"So shut your damn traps, do your jobs, and let the leaders take care of making the decisions."

No one spoke after that.

We spent the evening as we'd done all week—enjoying a delicious supper inside the bunker with a large crowd. Although I didn't see Arahm, I had a feeling he was hiding somewhere in the back, cooking up a storm. In a place like this, he probably now had access to all kinds of cooking equipment.

Probably even electric ones.

Our group returned to our hallway, some people more excited than others. I'd spent most of the week fighting flashbacks from Lutum, or trying to remind myself that the armed soldiers around us weren't going to suddenly start beating on someone.

The last thing I wanted to do was socialize.

So without a word, I went straight into my room. I didn't bother showering, and instead, fell straight into bed.

When I woke up again, I glanced over at the clock built into the wall. The red digits read, 3:04 *a.m.*

I wanted to go back to sleep, but I couldn't. I found myself thinking of Grandma's sweet, innocent face. Ever since I'd found out about her death, I'd pushed the thought away, knowing I had to manage my sorrow if I didn't want to drop my guard and get killed.

I couldn't be weak.

I couldn't break.

But as I lay there in the darkness, everything hit me at once.

She was gone. Forever. Even if we managed

to overtake the Elites and Lutum, I'd never see her again. I'd never feel her warm lips against my forehead or tiny frame against mine as she held me close. I wanted her back. Even if it meant living the rest of my life in Lutum. I'd do it.

I just wanted Grandma back.

I thought of Mother and how I'd been robbed of a potential relationship with her. I mourned what could have been more than what I'd lost, but it hurt all the same.

As I turned to my side, hot tears poured from my eyes and down my cheeks. Hugging my pillow, I wished it were Grandma. With my face buried in its soft, plush material, I cried until my head pounded and I thought I might throw up.

CHAPTER 9

Every morning, breakfast was served in the same hall as the one where we ate supper.

It was less formal, though. No one served food. Instead, people lined up to grab themselves a plate, as they had done in Ortus.

Today, however, things were different. As Undergrounders emerged from their rooms, it became apparent that they weren't planning on heading to their work posts after breakfast. Some still wore pajamas, while others were dressed in clean clothes that no one would wear to work outdoors.

I'd overhead some people talk about their *plans for the weekend*, though I wasn't sure what that meant.

"What's going on?" Sadie whispered.

I shrugged and made my way to the back door of our hallway. The moment we entered the central hub, Alvan stood up from his bright red chair and clasped his brown hands together. "Ah, there you are."

Behind us, more and more people came through, including Lyson, Lyla, and other faces I wasn't too familiar with. I searched around for Asako, but I couldn't find her, either. The last time I'd asked Alvan, he'd mentioned that she was being treated in the medical center.

What was most confusing was to see people exiting the dining hall with plates of food in their hands, only to return to their rooms.

Where were they going?

Hudson was the first to speak up. "What's going on?"

Alvan smiled politely. "It's the weekend, sir."

"Are weekends off?" Lyson asked.

Alvan smiled again. "Yes, of course."

Of course? He confirmed it as if it were obvious that everyone got weekends off. Back in Ortus, I recalled some people taking breaks on weekends, but it wasn't everyone—many people continued to work. We often lost valuable time to rainfall and storms, so it was no wonder people didn't want to waste their weekends away doing nothing when the weather was beautiful.

And as for the Champions—we never took time off. Sadie had made it clear that unless there was a severe storm, we were expected to train outside. Reina was the only one to authorize days off for recovery, and although I hadn't spent enough time in Ortus to receive a day off, I was told it occurred about once a month, for approximately four days straight.

"You are welcome to explore the bunker," Alvan said. "Otherwise, follow me, and I'll show you what activities we have to offer."

Activities. He made it sound like *fun.*

He led us toward the dining hall but took a left turn before entering—away from the stairwell to the courtyard—and led us down a series of narrow halls.

"We have several facilities down here," he said. "They're especially useful on days when we have storms. On weekends, the courtyard is used mostly by the children for playtime."

"So no one works on weekends?" I clarified.

Alvan looked at me like we were speaking different languages. "Absolutely not."

Smiles spread through our groups as Alvan brought us to a doorway that read *Activities* above it. It was carved in a slab of wood and looked out of place, almost as if a child had made it during a school project.

"I won't bring you to each individual area," Alvan said.

He moved out of the way when a group of young people wearing strange colorful suits brushed past him. Some even wore little rubberlike caps and held towels around their shoulders.

Sadie must have caught me making a sour face. "Those are swimsuits," she said. "Haven't you ever seen one?"

I couldn't answer. I was too weirded out by the little caps that made them look bald.

"We have an Olympic-sized swimming pool, a recreation center with weight and cardio machines, a basketball court, a shooting range—which is restricted access—a library—"

Lyson nudged me in the ribs, grinning.

A *library*.

I couldn't help but smile.

"An indoor playground," Alvan continued. He tapped his chin and stared at the high ceiling. "A sports field, though it isn't as popular as the basketball court." He crinkled his nose. "There are a few other things, but I'll let you explore them."

Before he could say another word, several people hurried past him and charged through the door. A clean smell swept through the open door, followed by the sound of countless people shouting and laughing. When the door slammed shut, everything went quiet again, and the overhead sign slanted to the right a bit, but it stayed in place.

"Well, go ahead," Alvan said, almost laughing.

Sadie was the next one to reach for the handle. "All right, let's check it out."

As I stepped forward to follow her through, Reina's voice caught me off guard. "Silver."

I flinched at the sound of my name and turned around. She stood against the hallway's concrete wall with her arms folded over her chest. Today, she wore blue pants—something I learned were referred to as jeans—and a gray button-up blouse. I wasn't used to seeing her wear something so casual. She was always in tactical gear. For the first time, her hair wasn't tied in a bun at the back of her head. Instead, she let it hang loose behind her back. Despite her new attire and hairdo, she didn't look any less intimidating.

"A word," she said.

I gulped.

Sadie looked back at me as the door began to close. I showed her a single finger, which was meant to translate to, *Give me a minute.* When the door closed, I wasn't sure she'd understood my sign language, but it didn't matter.

Reina—*General Reina*—wanted to speak with me, and there was no ignoring that.

As I moved closer, she watched me quietly. I squished myself against the wall as other groups came through, many of them our own people, and many others, Undergrounders.

The majority of them laughed together, which gave me hope that their resentment toward us was lessening.

"Elias has tasked me with forming a search group to explore the wastelands next week."

"What do you mean?" I asked. "For supplies?"

She nodded, waiting for the crowd to lessen. Eventually, everyone disappeared through the Activities door, and the space around us became quiet.

"Our population is putting strain on their resources. We can't wait months for more crops to grow. We need to find additional supplies as soon as possible—clothing, building materials, medical supplies, salt, anything."

I wasn't sure what I had to do with any of this. Did she expect me to go out there? I wasn't the one with the guns—Elias's people were. And why had he put Reina in charge of this mission? Didn't Elias and his people do this sort of thing all the time?

"And don't worry," she said. "Elias has several crossbows. I'll teach you how to use one before you go."

"Before I go?" I blurted. "Why am I going? Your other Champions have way more fighting experience than I do."

Reina tightened her arms across her chest and sighed. "It isn't up to me, Silver. Elias asked for you specifically."

I was speechless. Why would Elias want me going out there? Was this some sort of trick? Was he trying to get rid of me? Maybe the Woodfaces were still a threat—maybe their *tank* hadn't gotten rid of our enemies, after all.

"I don't see what good I'm going to do," I admitted. I didn't want to come across as weak or insecure, but the fact was, I'd only started training a few weeks ago. Some of these Champions, including Sadie and Reina, had been training for years.

"What about Sadie?" I asked.

"What about her?" Reina said.

"Will she be joining me?"

Reina shook her head. "Sadie still needs to recover. And this isn't a battle mission. You'll have some of Elias's soldiers with you."

It still didn't add up. "I don't get it," I said. "You're going to train me on how to use a crossbow just to send me out there along with Elias's soldiers? I don't even know this territory. His people do. Reina, this doesn't feel right. I'm not going to be of any use to whoever is leading this mission. I'll be added weight—"

"What? No," Reina said as if I'd misunderstood everything. "You aren't following anyone, Silver. You're *leading*."

CHAPTER 10

I hurried back to my room, my heart pounding.

Leading?

I didn't believe it. Elias was up to no good. Why would he have me lead a mission outside of the bunker after learning that everyone out there wanted me dead? This was a trap. It had to be.

I scanned my access card next to my door and hurried in, wanting nothing more than to be left alone with my thoughts. Maybe if I thought this through long enough, I'd figure out what his plan was. But right before my door swept closed, Sadie stuck her arm out, and the door reopened.

"Sadie," I said, surprised to see her.

What I really wanted to say was, *Not right now*, but I knew she was only concerned about me.

"What's going on?" she asked. "We were just

informed that there's a huge library down here. You have a day off. You're in your room." She crossed her arms and gave me her unimpressed look. "Something's up."

I was afraid if I told Sadie the truth, she'd be upset with Reina. Why would Reina come to me over Sadie? Then again, it hadn't been up to Reina. She'd made that quite clear. Elias was the one behind this.

"Come on, spit it out," Sadie said.

Her bold blue eyes made it impossible for me to hide the truth from her.

So I repeated what Reina had told me—every detail—until Sadie sat down on the edge of my bed and scratched the back of her head.

"I admit it's weird," she said.

I didn't respond.

"What are you going to do?"

"What choice do I have?" I said.

"You have several choices." She folded her arms. "You can go see Elias and ask him. You can stop pouting in your room and come have some fun with us. You can get excited that you'll be learning how to use a freaking crossbow."

She winked teasingly, as if on the verge of poking me hard in the ribs.

Sadie was right. Isolating in my room wasn't doing me any favors. At supper, I could very well speak with Elias and ask him to explain why he was doing this.

So I followed Sadie back to the Activities area in the bunker, trying to ignore the fact that in two days, I would be going aboveground to lead a group of fighters through the wastelands.

The thought of it made me sick, so I focused on admiring everything the Activities area had to offer.

Sadie gave me a tour, and I was most impressed with the indoor swimming pool. I'd never seen such clean-looking water before. It even looked blue. Sadie explained that the colored *liner* gave the illusion that the water was blue. Either way, it was beautiful.

Long ropes ran down the length of the pool, and attached to them were cylinder shapes floating on the surface of the water.

People of all ages and body shapes jumped into the water, laughing, and water splashed in every direction. Some wore bright orange puffs around their arms, and others swam freely. In the *shallow* end, as Sadie explained, parents played with their young toddlers, carrying them through the water and teaching them how to swim.

A strong chemical smell filled my nose, but I liked it. It smelled clean. Blue and green tiles sparkled beneath my boots. They looked wet and felt slippery. Most people walked around barefoot, which seemed like the more sensible thing to do.

Every time someone tried to run, an adult shouted at them, telling them to *walk*.

I imagined it had something to do with safety.

"Wanna go in?" Sadie asked.

I looked around. "I don't have a swimsuit."

She pointed at a booth in the corner where a woman sat behind a glass window. "Mrs. Loretta hands them out. If you can find one in your size, it's yours to keep. There aren't many left, though."

As luck would have it, Mrs. Loretta—a sweet woman with a thick accent—managed to find my size within a matter of minutes. She handed it to me with a smile so big her cheeks almost hid her eyes. The material felt stretchy and silky.

Sadie led me back into something called a changing room, where we switched into our new swimsuits. Mine was purple with two white stripes running down my sides. It looked cool, and I was thankful to have one.

My heart pounded hard as Sadie led me toward the deep end, where most of the adults swam.

"You're just going to jump in?" I asked.

How was I supposed to tell her that I didn't know how to swim? Every adult here seemed to be swimming just fine. Would she laugh at me? Ridicule me?

"Um, yeah," she said, on the verge of laughing. "I mean, unless you want to go swim with the kids over there, but kids tend to pee in water—"

"Pee?" I repeated.

She led me next to a big blue thing that people kept jumping off of.

I parted my lips, prepared to tell her I didn't know how to swim, when she shouted, "Last one to the end loses!" and shoved me in the water.

I flew through the air and landed on my back, slamming into the water which was neither cold nor warm. First, it pinched my skin, but within seconds, I began to sink, and then, the panic set in.

Water slipped into my nostrils and into my mouth, so I held my breath.

I blinked hard as my head dipped underneath the water. No matter how hard I kicked, it seemed impossible for me to return to the surface. What if I kicked too hard? Would I sink even faster? I looked around, my surroundings blurry and my eyes burning.

Above me was a bright light.

How could I get back up there? My heart pounded hard as I sank lower. My lungs began to ache, and all I wanted to do was inhale a deep breath, but I knew if I did, I'd pull water into my lungs.

Even my ears began to hurt. Why was there pressure like that?

I was so terrified that I wanted to yell for someone to come save me, but I couldn't scream.

Suddenly, two firm hands grabbed me by the waist and tugged on me. Awkwardly, someone pulled me back to the surface, but the movements were jagged, like the person was struggling to carry both of our weights. The second my head surfaced, I sucked so much air into my aching lungs that people turned to look at me.

The person brought me to the side of the pool, where I held on tightly to the ledge, coughing and trembling.

"What the hell is wrong with you?" Lyla asked.

I hadn't recognized her because her hair was so wet that it looked dark.

At first, I thought she was talking to me—accusing me of being an idiot for not knowing how to swim. But by the way she was glaring up at Sadie, I knew her words hadn't been directed at me at all.

Sadie's eyes were huge. With slanted brows, she slapped a hand over her mouth. "Silver... I-I'm so sorry. I thought you knew how to swim."

"She's from Lutum," Lyla said. "Where the hell would she have learned how to swim?"

Sadie dropped her chin to her chest. "I-I'm sorry. I wasn't thinking. I'm so sorry."

With that, she turned away and rushed back into the change room.

"Sadie!" I tried, but I started coughing again.

Lyla scowled at me furiously. "Don't chase after her. She doesn't deserve to be comforted. She almost got you killed."

I wasn't sure whether to tell Lyla to back off or thank her for saving me. So I did neither and stared at her, unable to say a word.

"Can you get out of the pool, or do you need help with that, too?"

Her words came out like she was annoyed for having saved my life.

When I didn't respond, she rolled her eyes. "Don't drown again, okay? I might not be around next time."

Then, she pushed off the side of the pool and zipped underneath the water like a fish.

I managed to pull myself out and return to the change room, where Sadie sat with her forehead in her palms. When I entered, my wet feet smacking the tiled floor, she glanced up at me.

"Silver, I'm so sorry. Honestly. I feel like a

moron.”

“You didn’t know,” I said. “It’s okay.”

“It’s not okay. I didn’t even realize you were drowning. I thought you were just playing around under the water. And I stood there like an idiot, laughing at you.”

She hung her head.

I reached for her shoulder but she pulled away. “Don’t try to console me. Stop being nice like that.”

“I’m not dead.”

She scowled at me. “You could have died.”

“But I didn’t.”

She breathed in sharply through her nose and leaned her head against the tiled wall.

“How about you stop pouting in here and do something productive?” I said.

When her scowl didn’t vanish, I got the feeling my joke wasn’t well-received. But when she caught my half smile, she smiled back.

“Like what?” she said.

“Like teach me how to swim.”

After a beat, she let out a big sigh and stood. “Fine, but let’s stick to the shallow end.”

CHAPTER 11

When suppertime rolled around, Elias was nowhere to be seen.

With a stern look and a squeeze to my forearm, Sadie reassured me that everything would be okay. I wanted to believe her, but I got the feeling she didn't even believe herself.

I considered speaking with Finn about it, but neither he nor Reina were present in the dining hall.

Where were the leaders? Discussing?

Dax no longer ate suppers with us. She spent most of her time with Mia. Even Danika seemed to be showing interest in a boy she'd met in the courtyard. I caught her smiling now and then, and when I asked her about it, she gave me a shy smile and shrug, which wasn't very Danika-like. I never knew her to be shy.

Maybe that was precisely what our two colonies needed—to be united through love.

Although Rose apparently hadn't found a love interest yet, she seemed chipper every day. Getting to work with Arahm making food for the entire society seemed to have reinvigorated her. I'd seen her interact with Arahm's children more than once, and although she didn't speak, she didn't seem to have a problem getting her message across to them with all sorts of gestures.

Despite all the happiness around me, I went to bed with a sense of dread that evening.

When I woke up the next morning, I wasn't even sure I'd slept. I got dressed and quietly exited my room before anyone could see me leaving.

As instructed by Reina, I returned to the Activities area.

When I arrived, Reina stood leaning against the wall, watching me. Was I late? Why wasn't she saying anything?

"I thought you said six," I said.

Looking smug, she pushed herself off the wall. "I did."

Her long black hair swayed behind her back as she swept the door open. I followed her in, eyeballing the sign above me and hoping it wouldn't fall square on my head. It didn't look to be very well attached.

We walked past the pool area and went straight to the back toward an ominous door.

The smallest of windows sat at eye level, though it looked dark inside. Next to the door was a slim metal sign that read, *Shooting Range*.

Using her access card, Reina unlocked the door and led me through. We walked through several series of doors that seemed to have been unnecessarily added, but I imagined they served a purpose. Maybe it was to ensure no children got inside. Or, maybe it was to keep noise out.

We walked past a large, rectangular room with dark and damaged concrete walls. At the far end paper targets appeared to be dangling from cables. What good was *paper*? Where was the wood? And the straw?

Closer to me were stalls divided by thin black walls. Did people stand within each stall to shoot their weapons?

When Reina kept walking, I looked back. "Aren't those the targets?"

She cocked a brow at me like I knew nothing. "Yeah, for guns. I told you you're training on a crossbow."

We moved through another set of doors and landed in a room that reminded me a bit of Ortus. Everything was made of wood—the walls, the floor, and even the ceiling. At the very back were various targets—some round, others square and small, and some carved into the shape of human figures. They were all positions at various distances from what appeared to be the shooting line—a large red stripe that ran across the floor.

Reina disappeared behind another door, but she moved so quickly that I got the feeling she didn't want me to follow. So I waited until she returned with a strange weapon that looked like a combination of a gun and a bow.

It was entirely black and although I couldn't tell what it was made of, it looked durable. Under the weapon were two arrows attached, but unlike the arrows I'd used in Ortus, these were shorter, perfectly straight, and had red fletching that didn't look like feathers.

"This is a crossbow," Reina said fondly.

She handed it to me—it looked like she wanted to keep it for herself—and I was taken aback by its weight. It wasn't overly heavy, but I'd expected something lighter for a weapon. It was also larger than I had envisioned. I twirled it around a few times, inspecting every inch of it.

"That's your stock..." She pointed at the back of it. "Your scope, your string, your barrel, the cables, your riser, your foregrip, and of course, your arrows, which are called bolts."

I blinked hard as she pointed at all the parts.

"Few basic rules. Never dry fire. Watch your fingers when you cock. And never point a crossbow at anyone unless you plan to fire. I don't care if it's loaded or not. It's a good habit to have."

She took it back from me and went on to show me other parts. I knew I'd never remember half of what she was teaching me, but I did my best to pay attention. When she showed me how to load it—or cock it, as she referred to it—I wondered if I could even replicate her actions. She loaded a bolt, then placed the crossbow facedown on the floor. When it came time to pull the string back, her arms trembled a bit.

Raising the crossbow, she took aim and fired toward the targets. It made a loud yet brief snapping sound, and the bolt landed in the back wall, its strange fletching on an angle.

"Haven't shot one of these bad boys in years. We had a few in Ortus, but they broke." She handed it to me. "Your turn."

It took a few tries, and a lot of strength, to finally get the string loaded. As I stood, aiming at one of my targets without really knowing what I was doing, she pointed at the scope. "Use this. And keep your arms up." She fixed my stance. "There you go. Try to aim your sight on your target."

I did as she instructed, and when I pressed down on the trigger as she'd done, I twitched when the bolt flew out. The blast was powerful—more powerful than any bow I'd ever fired.

Although I missed my shot, the power of this thing was exciting.

"You like?" she said, no doubt catching a glimpse of my grin.

"Yeah," I admitted.

She dragged a box of bolts to my feet. "Well, keep practicing. I'll see you in a bit."

She left, and I stood alone in the dimly lit range, excited at the idea of mastering a crossbow. I knew I wouldn't become great in only a day, but I got the feeling that the scope would make things a whole lot easier for me.

By my seventh shot, my hands and shoulders began to ache. It wasn't from the firing, but from the cocking. I rolled my shoulders back, trying to soothe the pain, when a distant sound caught my attention.

It was like a snapping or a soft explosion, though it sounded muffled in here.

The sound emerged over and over again, so I followed it to the door. I pressed my ear against the cool metal, hearing it more distinctly this time. Curious, I reached for the door handle, twisted it, and slowly pulled.

But right as the door creaked open, the explosive sounds blared out so loudly I thought my eardrums might burst. So I slammed the door shut again and stepped away.

What the heck was that?

I'd never heard anything so loud before.

How was I supposed to even get out of here with all those explosive sounds? They were so loud that even if I'd thrown my hands over my ears, I wasn't so sure it would help. They continued, banging and banging as I stood alone with my crossbow at my feet.

Suddenly, all sound stopped, and I blinked hard, staring at the door.

I was prepared to peer through again when it opened on its own, and in popped a man's face I didn't recognize. He had a short red and gray beard and some sort of headset over his curly locks and ears.

"It's the girl," he shouted behind him.

"What girl?" someone else said.

Out of nowhere, the door kicked open and the red-haired man almost fell flat on his face. He stumbled into the room with me, and behind him stood Jared, glaring at me with his intense black eyes.

Pouting his lips, he elevated his freshly shaven chin. "What are *you* doing here?"

"I-I was asked to train," I said.

He glanced down at my crossbow. "With my father's crossbow?"

My heart pounded hard. I didn't like the idea of being alone, cornered by men I didn't know. Especially by Jared.

"It was given to me to practice," I said. "I–I don't mind using a different one if you have one."

His glare didn't soften. Instead, he sucked on his teeth, inspecting me from head to toe.

"Who let you inside?" he asked. "You people aren't supposed to have access to our shooting range."

I didn't want to give him Reina's name. The last thing I wanted was to cause trouble for her. So instead, I told him the truth and left her out of it.

"Elias asked me to train," I said.

Jared's pale lips curled into a venomous smile. "Of course, he did." He turned to his men and laughed. The redhead laughed with him the most, like he was trying hard to boost Jared's ego.

"Leave the crossbow and get the hell out of my range," Jared said.

I wanted to argue that this was Elias's orders, but I had no one here to defend me if things got ugly. I was alone and outnumbered. With a bowed head, I inched past him and walked through a crowd of a dozen large men. They, too, wore strange headsets, which I got the feeling were meant to protect their ears from the loud shooting sounds.

I spotted a few guns lying on shelves but quickly looked away, afraid one of the men might decide to grab one if they saw me eyeballing the weapons. As I reached for the first exit door, Reina pushed her way through, startling me.

"Where are you going?" she asked. "Your training isn't over."

I didn't have to say anything for her to see what was going on. She searched the group of men, gave me a stern look, and said, "Come on. We'll come back when they're gone."

Jared slowly marched his way toward us, one heavy step at a time. "You won't come back at all." His rumbly voice sounded throughout the shooting range.

Reina stopped walking, closed her eyes, and sucked in a deep breath through flaring nostrils. I expected her to either shout something back or to bottle it all in and keep walking, but she grabbed my arm, twirled me around, and marched us right back toward Jared and his men.

He looked as shocked as I felt. His eyes rounded, but only briefly. He met her halfway inside the range, towering over her.

"What didn't you understand?" he said. "I told you to get out."

Reina grabbed her hips, puffed out her chest, and stared him cold in the face. She was much shorter than Jared, but the anger in her eyes proved she wasn't afraid of him. "This range doesn't belong to you. If you want exclusive, privileged access, I suggest you take it up with the leader of this place. In case you forget, that isn't *you*."

His jaw muscles popped, and a few of his men stepped forward as if waiting for an order to strike Reina down.

Folds formed across Jared's forehead as he no doubt played out various scenarios in his mind. Was he going to hit her? To forcefully drag her out? Or, would he shut his mouth and walk away? I didn't know this man, but judging by the encounter I'd had with him in the dining hall, I knew he wasn't afraid to hit anyone, including a woman.

Despite my trembling knees, I clenched my fists. If things got physical, we didn't stand a chance. But Reina didn't seem to care. She wasn't backing down. It was almost like she welcomed him to try something.

Suddenly, Jared glanced up at one of his men and nodded.

I didn't have time to interpret what this wordless message was. Without warning, the man grabbed Reina by the arm and pulled hard, trying to drag her out.

But she wasn't having it.

In one swift motion, she slid her foot across the floor in the shape of a half circle, kicking the man's legs out from under him. As he fell to the ground, she snatched two of his fingers, yanking them back hard the moment he landed on his side.

She stared at him wide-eyed, threatening to break them without speaking.

The man winced, baring his rotting teeth at us and tapping his chest as if to say, *Please stop.*

She pulled down harder and the man cried out. "P-p-please!"

The man nearest to Reina took a step toward her, and without even letting go of the other man's fingers, she whipped a sharp knife out from her belt and aimed it at the second intruder.

"Take another step, and I'll cut them off."

The second man backed off.

"If you want to be my enemy," Reina said, "I'll treat you like my enemy. I prefer we keep things civil, but I'll respect your wishes if you choose otherwise."

With tight lips, she glared at Jared and breathed out hard through her flared nostrils. Although I didn't want to believe it, something in her eyes told me that if Jared didn't back down, she might follow through with her threat.

It was a primal side to her that I'd never seen before—almost as if Jared had triggered some past trauma in her.

No one moved, likely not knowing how to

respond to her threat. Had Jared never been confronted like this before? My teeth chattered as adrenaline coursed through me.

Out of nowhere, Jared smiled and loosened his stance. His men did the same, lowering their balled fists and relaxing their shoulders.

"Come on, boys," Jared said, laughing. "The lady wants the range. Let's give her the range."

Smiling, he walked out slowly, and his men followed, staring at us with such contempt that I knew this was far from over.

Reina released her grip on the man's fingers, and he pulled away, grumbling something to himself. He pressed his injured fingers against his chest and tumbled out of the shooting range, along with the rest of Jared's men.

CHAPTER 12

"What's wrong with you?" Sadie asked.

I jabbed my fork into my potatoes, monitoring the front of the dining hall. "Elias still isn't here."

Danika shoved a piece of potato into her mouth. "Why do you care where Elias is?" A few bits fell back out into her plate.

I shook my head dismissively. I hadn't told anyone else about tomorrow's plans—about how I was supposed to lead a group of Champions and fighters into the wastelands to find resources. And why hadn't Elias shown up at dinner the last two evenings? Was he trying to avoid me?

"You're spiraling," Sadie said, grabbing my arm.

Only then did I realize it was trembling.

"What's going on?" Danika asked.

"I'm leaving the bunker tomorrow," I finally admitted.

Hudson, along with a few others at our table, turned to look at me.

"To scavenge for resources," I clarified.

Hudson didn't look bothered by it. He stretched his injured hand at the end of his sling, watching his fingers. "You have some of our people going with you, don't you?"

I nodded.

"Then you'll be fine," he said.

Sadie glared at him. "She doesn't need people to protect her."

Hudson leaned back and waved his good arm as a way of quickly apologizing. "You got me wrong. I'm not saying she needs to be saved. You look stressed about the whole thing, so you want to talk to Elias about it. I'm betting you don't understand why they're sending you out there when they have their own people."

Hudson was more intuitive than I gave him credit for.

He shrugged one muscular shoulder and continued, "But if they're also sending some of our people, then I don't think it's a trap." He paused, watching me carefully. "I mean, if that's what you were thinking."

I forced a smile. "Thanks, Hudson."

Without smiling back, he jabbed his fork into his plate, grabbing so many potatoes they broke off his fork. "Don't mention it."

I finished supper, trying to repeat Hudson's words in my head over and over again. Maybe he was right. If this was a trap, why send some of our people into the mission?

I barely spoke to anyone for the rest of the night. Instead, I went straight to sleep, hoping tomorrow's plans might change.

A soft knocking sound pulled me out of my dream, and I sat upright in bed.

I waited. Maybe I had imagined it.

Again, the knock echoed. I certainly hadn't imagined it. Groggy and blurry-eyed, I made my way to the door and pressed the red button.

The door swept open and Reina stood on the other side. "Morning, sunshine."

She handed me what looked to be coffee in a sky blue ceramic mug.

"I don't like coffee," I said.

She scoffed as if I'd lost my mind. "How many times have you tried it? Once? Coffee's an acquired taste." She handed it to me again. "Here."

She forced the mug into my hands. "And I brought you this." She then handed me what looked to be a muffin wrapped in a napkin.

"Is this breakfast?" I asked.

She nodded. "We're going to the parking

lot, not the dining hall, so you won't have time to grab breakfast with everyone."

"Reina—" I said, prepared to ask her more about this mission, but she jerked her head sideways as a way of saying, *Follow me*, and turned around.

Rather than moving toward the central hub, she led us down the opposite end of the hallway, through the door we'd crossed when we first arrived in the bunker.

The next thing I knew, I was standing in the parking lot.

As we entered, several other people stood around a sea green vehicle with huge wheels and black windows. The machine looked impenetrable. I wondered if bullets could even damage this thing.

Everyone wore the same outfit Jared often walked around sporting—a thick black material with hard protective plates and black boots to match. There were six of them in total—four men and two women. Three of the men were Elias's people, while the other man and the two women were ours. I'd seen them in Ortus's fighting grounds, but I'd never introduced myself.

"Get changed," Reina ordered, pointing at a folded black uniform sitting on top of the vehicle. On the floor, next to the massive wheels, were matching black boots like everyone else was wearing.

I looked down at my feet and at the boots Sadie had given me in Ortus. "What's wrong with mine?"

"Are they steel toe?" Reina asked.

Steel toe?

I crinkled my nose, and a few of the men laughed. I wasn't sure if they were laughing at me, or at the face I'd made.

"You'd know if they were," one of them said. He kicked his foot hard against the vehicle's wheel. It made a *clunk* sound, and he didn't wince or make a pained face.

Reina raised her eyebrows at me, which I knew meant, *Go on, do what I told you to do.*

She pointed at an open door on the side wall. Although dark inside, it looked to be a bathroom. I went inside, changed, and came back out looking like everyone else. Reina moved toward me, grabbed my hair, and tied it back into a bun at the base of my skull.

"Better," she said.

I reached for it. It felt weird. I'd never tied my hair like this before, but it was nice to not have it in my face.

"Here." She handed me the same crossbow I'd trained with.

"I know you're sore from all the training," she said, "but if anything happens out there, trust me, you won't be thinking about how sore you are."

I nodded and grabbed the weapon.

At the same time, a strange and brief buzzing sound resonated nearby. I must have jumped back three feet; Elias's people didn't seem bothered by it. Instead, they laughed at me and our Champions, who had clearly panicked as much as I had.

The vehicle next to me seemed to be rumbling, and it was only then that I realized it must have been turned *on*.

The black window at the front suddenly slid down, revealing a man with overly white teeth and bright red sunglasses. Blond facial hair ran down the sides of his face, but it looked like it was just starting to grow in. Either that, or he didn't easily grow a beard. He smiled at me like he'd enjoyed watching me jump back, then smacked the side of the vehicle and shouted, "Everyone, inside the *rover*!"

A rover, I thought, standing still as everyone else reached for handles and started opening doors.

Reina poked me in the back, urging me to get going. As I prepared to climb into the back of the rover, she grabbed my wrist and said, "Silver, you're leading, remember? Get in the front."

I wanted to burst out and tell her that this made no sense, but what would have been the point? Besides, this vehicle looked solid, which made me feel safe. Maybe I'd be okay. So I did as I was told and climbed into the front.

The seats were surprisingly comfortable and unlike anything I'd ever sat in before. When Reina closed the door next to me, it made a loud *thump* and her figure darkened instantly as if the lights had been turned out.

I grazed my finger across the window, trying to understand why it wasn't clear like all the other glass I'd seen.

"Tint," said the man next to me.

I turned to him.

"The windows," he clarified. "They're tinted. They're dark so no one can see who's inside."

When I didn't answer, he said, "You ready?"

He looked at me over his bright red sunglasses and grinned. What did he have to be so happy about? He slid his fingers across the black, shiny platform in front of us. "Dashboard."

I stared at the glossy surface. It looked like someone had recently oiled it.

"Hood." He pointed outside the rover, at the front. "Center console." Another point of his finger.

While I appreciated the lesson, I wasn't sure if he was doing it to actually teach me, or to make me look stupid.

"Wheel," he said at last. "It controls the tires. You know, those big black things you saw outside."

Behind me, a few of his friends snickered.

"James, let's just go," said one of the female fighters.

James pushed his sunglasses back up the bridge of his nose, sucked on his teeth, and reached for a button on the center console. It was the largest button there was—a bright blue circle that lit up when he pressed down on it.

At once, natural light flooded the oversized space as massive doors opened at the back. Just like in Olympus's pillars, the doors slid upward, curving along with the ceiling until completely flat.

"That's a seatbelt," he said, pointing at something next to my shoulder. "Grab it and click it in here."

I did as instructed, clicking the little metal piece into place.

Without warning, James pressed something else and my head slammed backward into my seat. It made my heart skip a beat and my palms became instantly clammy. Beside my window was what looked like a small mirror. In it, Reina's dark figure stood in the distance, shrinking in size we sped up a ramp and toward what felt like the sky.

"Hold on," James said.

I wanted to yell at him to stop. Why was he going so fast? And why were we aimed at the clouds? Could this thing fly?

Suddenly, when we came blasting out of the parking lot, a huge knot formed in my stomach.

Were we even touching the ground anymore?

I glanced sideways to spot grass below—far below. We were in the air!

But within seconds, we came down hard and the rover bounced. It made my head jerk forward, then back again, and James let out a laugh so loud it filled up the entire vehicle.

The other guys laughed, but the Champions in the back didn't look impressed. They watched me with huge eyes, almost as if waiting for me to say something.

I didn't—I couldn't. I was just as terrified as they were.

"Sorry," James said, still chuckling. "That's my favorite part out of the entire ride."

He moved his knee over and the vehicle suddenly came to an abrupt stop, sending me forward again. The seatbelt across my chest stopped me from hitting my face on the dashboard.

"See why that's important?" he said, nodding toward the dashboard.

My heart pulsated inside my neck.

"Show me how to control this thing," I said through clenched teeth.

"Excuse me?" he said. "I'm the driver."

"Not anymore," I said. "Show me how. Elias put me in charge, which means I'm driving."

"Silver," James said, his smile vanishing. "It takes months to learn how to properly—"

"If you want to keep driving, then stop acting like a five-year-old and just drive," I said.

Everyone inside the rover went quiet.

"All right, all right." He raised a hand in submission. "I was only trying to have a little fun. You don't have to be a buzzkill."

Buzzkill. I'd never heard that term before, but I got the impression it meant someone who liked to suck the fun out of everything. James had a warped sense of what was *fun.*

"Where to?" he asked, composing himself.

I stared at the open fields, disoriented. Where had we even come from? When I looked behind me, the parking lot was nowhere to be seen. Had James already closed the door? All that remained was grass, dirt, and trees.

But then, I spotted the forest—the same forest we'd traveled along when we first came here. I knew that going back toward Ortus made no sense. If we wanted to gather supplies from fallen cities, we had to explore new places.

"Where have you guys explored?" I asked.

James scoffed. "Everywhere." He pointed behind us, to the right, and even toward Ortus. "There are a few fallen cities around here. We always go to the same places. Sure, we find new treasures every time, but supplies are running low. We haven't found a new place in years."

"Who usually decides where you explore?" I asked.

James took off his sunglasses, revealing yellow-green eyes unlike anything I'd ever seen. At first, I thought maybe something was wrong with them. But as he squinted and pointed through the rover windows, I knew he had no trouble seeing with them. Around his unique eyes were golden eyelashes that made them stand out even more.

"Whoever's in your seat," he admitted.

"Who usually sits here?" I asked.

He shrugged. "Usually one of Jared's men."

The way his words came out told me he didn't enjoy being bossed around by Jared's men.

"They know these lands better than anyone since they're always out. I'm surprised Elias let us go scavenging at all without one of Jared's men. Jared's been the one running those missions lately."

"Maybe it has to do with Jared's behavior," I said coldly.

No one said anything. I wasn't sure if they were afraid to speak badly about Elias's brother, or if they were shocked that I wasn't afraid to do so.

"Where do you guys think we should go?" I asked.

I craned my neck to look at everyone in the back of the rover. They seemed taken aback to even be asked the question, like no one had ever cared to get their opinion. Within seconds, they started bickering, pointing in every direction through the dark windows.

"That's insane," someone said.

"Is it? It's one of the only places we haven't gone."

I spun around in my seat. "Where?"

Everyone froze, staring at me, until the largest man in the vehicle said, "Across the river."

I thought back to the old man in Finn's kitchen, and how he'd pointed at the map and told us about a place called Port Williamson. It was near this bunker, only, it sat across the river. And now, with the destroyed bridge, there was no getting across.

"Is there another bridge?" I asked.

James turned his head to the side, his red frames looking pink as the sun began to rise above the horizon. "Not exactly."

His mischievous smile returned, and I got

the feeling he had another plan in mind—
something dangerous.

CHAPTER 13

There's a reason Jared said no to your plan," said the woman sitting at the far back of the rover.

James didn't seem to care what she thought. "I'm telling you," he said. "This'll work."

I stared at the crumbled bridge, trying to envision James's idea. But it sounded insane. What if the plan failed? What if we crashed into the river?

"I'll show you." James stepped out of the rover and slammed the door shut.

I followed him, making my way over to the broken bridge. Pieces of wood, cement, and metal lay against the river's edge, attracting moss and bubbles. It looked filthy, which told me the bridge had collapsed long ago.

James pointed at the material as the others joined us with their large black guns. I hadn't brought my crossbow with me, and I hoped that wasn't a mistake.

"We can use these metal beams," James said. "And that cement. It'll hold. I have a few tools in the rover, too. Once we get to the other side, we can do the same thing over there."

No one else seemed convinced.

"And what if it doesn't hold?" one of the men asked. "You'll get us all killed."

"Worse, you'll lose the rover and Jared will kill you," someone else said.

James scoffed like he didn't care what Jared thought.

"They want resources," James said. "And Silver here's the first team leader to ever ask for our opinions. We've never had a say out here. Don't you want more of that?"

His friends nodded.

"So how about we all work together and come back with something worth bragging about?" he said. "Maybe that way, they'll let us scavenge more often."

He glanced my way, the morning sun making his already pale face look translucent.

His idea wasn't without a huge risk. But Elias's people had already explored most of these lands. It was worth trying, wasn't it?

James stared at me, likely sensing my hesitation. "Look, we don't have to do this. We can go out farther, if you prefer. There could be other places we haven't found yet. It's up to you."

As terrifying as it sounded to fly over the river, it was also the best idea I'd heard in a long time. I'd experienced the way the rover had jumped through the air when James sped out of the bunker. With the right *ramp* in place, as James had called it, getting to the other side wouldn't be hard. All we had to do was drive fast.

"Are you in?" he asked, a grin stretching his freckled face. "Oh, she's in. Look at that. She's smiling." He pointed at my lips. "I think she's in."

"Yeah," I said. "Let's do it."

Smacking his hands together, he started ordering people around. "Adu, grab those concrete blocks. Westin, you get those metal beams."

Adu, a thin man with creamy white skin, wide-set eyes, and jet-black hair, did as instructed and started collecting concrete blocks. Although he didn't look very strong, he didn't seem to have a problem lifting the heavy blocks.

Westin—a tall, dark-skinned man with muscles almost as big as Jayun's—followed Adu and started digging through the bridge's debris for metal beams. It was no wonder James had assigned him to do the heavy lifting. The guy was huge.

"The rest of you, grab whatever you can," James said.

Everyone jumped in, pulling out whatever they could from the water. When I reached for a plank of wood, my foot slipped on a muddy slope, and Westin caught my arm.

"You okay?" he asked.

I nodded. "Thanks."

Once we had all of our supplies in place, James disappeared in the back of the rover and returned with tools I'd never seen before. They looked electronic. One in particular looked like a gun. He aimed it at the sky, pressed a button, and made the tip spin with a loud zipping noise.

"You got the right screws for this?" Westin asked.

James gave him a dull look and raised a clear bag full of narrow silver bits.

Hours later, we finished the ramp. It was easily twice the width of the rover and seemed sturdy. To prove it, James ran on top and jumped up and down as if trying to stomp his feet through the sheets of metal. "Come on up," he said.

A few others went up, jumping as hard as they could.

The ramp didn't budge at all.

James flashed me a set of pearly whites. "Are we ready?"

I wasn't so sure I was, but at the same time,

I was excited at the idea of venturing where no one else had gone before. Was it risky? Absolutely. For all we knew, enemies might be waiting for us on the other side. But strangely, I felt safer traveling unexplored lands as opposed to sticking on this side, where we had already been targeted by armed men several weeks prior. And then there was also the risk of the Woodfaces. What proof did we have that there weren't more of them out there?

I stretched my back, sore from all the lifting. "As soon as we reach the other side, we need to build another one."

James laughed. "What's the hurry?"

"We need an escape route if things go bad," I said.

His smile vanished and he nodded. "Sounds good to me."

He jogged down the large ramp and the others followed.

"All right, folks, let's do this thing!" James strutted his way back to the rover.

Everyone got in and James turned the rover back on. To my surprise, we started moving backward, not forward. I snapped my head from side to side, looking outside. Was I imagining things?

James faced me for a moment. "Vehicles can go forward or backward. See this?" He pointed at a leathery vertical stick between us.

"This is how you control it."

He let his fingers dangle over the nob at the end of the stick, which now sat next to a big red R.

I assumed it was meant to signify, *Rear driving*, but I couldn't be sure.

We zoomed backward for yards until I could barely see the ramp anymore.

James stopped the car and shifted the stick to the letter D.

"What are you doing with your feet?" I asked, noting how he'd shifted his knee over again.

"Using the pedals," he said. He leaned back like that would somehow help me see through the darkness near his feet, but it didn't. I had to lean over to his side to see what he was pointing at. "That's the brake pedal, and that's the gas pedal, even though this technically doesn't have gas." He paused. "Gas means *go*." He let his glasses slip down the bridge of his nose and stared at me with his orange-yellow eyes. "If we succeed today, maybe you'll get to come out with us again, and I can show you how to drive this thing."

I smiled. "I'd like that."

"I'm going to speed up now, and it might get scary, but we have to do this fast," he warned.

I appreciated the warning this time around.

He looked up into a small mirror hanging

from the rover's ceiling. "You guys ready?"

My Champions remained quiet, but the others shouted things like, "Yeah!" and "Let's do it!"

With that, James slammed his foot onto the other pedal and my head jerked backward, slamming into the headrest.

We took off at incredible speed, and the rover bounced around gently as we crossed the uneven terrain. Although my heart pounded hard against the seatbelt and my stomach was queasy, part of me enjoyed it.

I'd never traveled this fast in my life. It was exhilarating and I couldn't wait to tell Sadie all about it.

As we moved faster and faster, and up ahead, the ramp became bigger, I found myself smiling.

And then I realized that as much fun as I was having, things were about to get very real. In a few seconds, we would be flying over the river and landing on the other side. And that was only if everything went well.

Considering this had never been done before, we couldn't be certain it would actually work.

"Wooo!" James shouted.

Around us, the scenery turned into a giant green blur.

The ramp seemed to be moving toward us,

even though I knew we were the ones moving.

Almost there.

I held my breath.

"Hold on!" James shouted.

Suddenly, a powerful jolt shook the rover and my body flung forward, against the seatbelt. At the same time, a loud clanking sound rang out around us, followed by loud rattling. It didn't last long—maybe only a second—but it made me wonder if perhaps the ramp beneath us had shattered into a thousand pieces.

The rattling stopped as quickly as it had started, and then, my stomach sank. I didn't appreciate the feeling, but I knew what it meant as I'd felt it earlier that day—we were no longer touching the ground. I pressed my face against my tinted window, staring in awe as we floated across the river.

A smile cracked my face as I watched the current continue to flow wildly beneath us. Although I knew we weren't touching the water, I feared we might land in it.

But I didn't have time to dwell on that thought.

By the time I blinked again, we were coming down fast toward the other side of the river.

"Hold on!" James shouted.

The front of the car slammed down into the ground and my body rocked forward, stopped once more by the seatbelt across my chest.

In my peripheral, James reached for his glasses as they flew off his face, but he missed them and they slid across the dashboard.

Next, the back tires landed, and the rover bounced around a few more times before he slammed the brakes, bringing us to a complete stop.

Were we okay? Were we alive? Silence filled the rover, and then, everyone burst out into laughter.

With his hands around the steering wheel, James turned to me, his mouth split into a huge grin.

"You did it," I said, still in shock over what had just happened.

He laughed loudly, then reached for my shoulder and shook me. "We did it!"

CHAPTER 14

James smacked the hood of the rover. "Not a dent."

Everyone kept laughing and talking about our jump. Even the Champions shook with excitement, pointing animatedly at the river and recounting how hard we'd landed.

James made his way to the back of the rover again and extracted the same tools he'd used to secure the first ramp. "All right, guys and gals, let's repeat the process." He nodded at me. "Silver's orders."

Everyone worked together again to build our return ramp. James suggested we move it over several yards to avoid crashing into our first ramp. It was a smart idea, and I agreed with it.

By the time we finished, everyone was tired.

"What do you think Jared will say when he finds out?" Westin asked, stretching his huge, muscular back. He grabbed a water bottle from the rover's open back door and everyone followed suit.

Their female fighter chugged hers back, gasping for air as she finished the bottle.

I worried that with all the energy we'd put into preparing our route, we wouldn't have much left to scavenge the wastelands.

"Who cares what Jared thinks?" James said.

The other fighters eyeballed each other.

The Champions, on the other hand, looked at me, likely curious to hear what I had to say about Jared.

"He's Elias's brother, isn't he?" I asked.

James wiped water from his pale freckled lips and nodded.

"What's the story behind that?" I asked. "It looks like Jared is jealous that Elias is in charge."

"He is," James said, matter-of-factly. "All he does is intimidate people who don't want what he wants. And for some reason, a lot of people seem to agree with him."

Adu wiped beads of sweat from his forehead and pushed dark hair out of his face. "Jared thinks Elias is too soft. I don't think that makes him right or wrong."

James rolled his eyes. "Adu, always the diplomat."

I wasn't sure what James meant by that.

Adu shrugged his padded shoulders. "What? I only speak the truth. Jared puts his people above all else—"

A few others gave him the stink eye, likely warning him to choose his next words carefully.

"Why does everyone tiptoe around words?" Adu asked. "The fact is, you're a stranger." He pointed at me, then at my Champions. "You all are. We don't really know you. I don't understand why Jared is being scrutinized for wanting to be cautious."

James gave me an apologetic look, but I didn't mind hearing what Adu had to say. He was only sharing his opinion, and the truth was, we *were* strangers. We *were* outsiders. At least to them. So I understood wanting to be cautious and certainly didn't fault anyone for that. Jared, however, was downright rude and obnoxious.

I didn't tell them about what had happened in the shooting range; there was no point in adding charcoal to the fire, as Grandma used to say. Instead, I finished the water James had kindly given me and placed the bottle back into a cardboard box at the back of the rover.

I glanced up at the sky and the sun's position. "Let's travel north, away from the river." I aimed my words at James. "I'm sure you and your team have already traveled the length of the river, so if there had been anything worth seeing on this side, you would have spotted it."

James agreed, then brushed past Adu and gave him a nasty look.

"Are you all okay to keep moving?" I asked.

Everyone nodded and we made our way back inside the rover.

James pressed on his pedal and the rover moved forward fast, filling me with that same feeling of exhilaration. What I loved most of all about this rover was that I wasn't afraid to get shot at with an arrow. If we happened to come across an enemy, it didn't matter. It wasn't like their arrows could penetrate the rover's exterior.

Bullets, on the other hand, I wasn't so sure.

We sped through the vast field, flattening tall blades of grass as we moved. Some areas were denser than others, making it difficult to see far ahead. A few trees stood tall, but not nearly enough to be considered a forest. James simply swerved around them, avoiding both their trunks and their far-reaching roots.

The farther we traveled, the taller the vegetation seemed to become, so James slowed down.

I watched the center console as we moved, where a screen showed what looked to be a compass. James seemed to be making an effort to keep the needle facing north. Every time the needle shifted slightly, he adjusted his steering wheel and recentered our course.

"Keep your eyes open," he said. "We don't know this place."

I searched through the tall vegetation, hoping to catch a glimpse of something.

"You sure this thing can't get stuck?" I asked.

James grinned at me. "Not with these tires. We'd have to fall into a pretty steep ditch to get stuck."

That put me at ease. With all the tall plants around us, I was afraid they'd get tangled in the wheels. Fortunately, this didn't happen.

We traveled for miles as the sun made its descent in the sky.

"We can travel a few more miles," James said. "Then, we have to turn around."

"How come?" I asked.

He pointed at something in front of his steering wheel. "We're almost at half a tank."

"What does that mean?" I asked.

He laughed—a deep, amused laugh that made me feel a bit foolish. "Did you think this thing could operate forever?"

I didn't know how to answer that. It wasn't like I'd given it any thought.

"Like a horse, this rover can't keep on moving forever. Horses need to eat. They need rest. This thing needs energy. It used to run on something called gasoline, or gas, but we ran out of that ages ago. At least that's what my dad tells me. So this thing was converted to run only on electricity. We plug it in, and the battery fills up. A full charge gives us about six hundred miles."

My eyes almost jumped out of their sockets. "Six hundred miles?"

He seemed entertained by my reaction. "A lot, huh?"

I was too stunned to even respond.

"So that's what limits us," he said. "We can only travel about three hundred miles before we have to turn around. We've been wanting to go over the river for years. But Jared always said we could find whatever we needed on this side, and that it was no use risking lives to explore those lands."

"He's wrong," I said. "There could be so much out here we don't know about."

"I agree," James said.

We sat in silence for a while longer as we continued our journey. We drove over a few large rocks, which startled me every time. I wondered if I'd ever get used to the feeling of being in a vehicle.

James stared straight ahead with his sunglasses tight on his face. Every few seconds, he tilted his nose down a bit, and I knew he was looking at the energy reservoir, or whatever it was called. We didn't want to wait until exactly the halfway point, because if anything went wrong on the way back, we risked getting stranded.

"We should—" he said, but out of nowhere, there was a loud crashing sound, and something threw me forward, making me smash my eyebrow against the rover's dashboard.

CHAPTER 15

s everyone okay?" James asked through rapid breaths.

I reached for my eyebrow and touched warm liquid. When I pulled my fingers back, they were bright red.

"What the hell happened?" asked Westin. He leaned forward, his big head between James and me, and searched the rover's hood.

I did the same by unclipping my seatbelt and stretching over the dashboard. What had we hit? There was nothing there.

"I-I don't know," James admitted. "I can't see anything. It just stopped the rover."

"Maybe this is a trap," Adu said. He tapped his hairless chin and squinted through the front window. "It would be idiotic to step out. For all we know, explosive devices are waiting right below. One wrong step—"

"There aren't any explosive devices!" James said. "Don't be ridiculous."

"It doesn't sound ridiculous," said the female Champion.

"Emma, don't be like that," said the other Champion.

Emma gave her fellow Champion a nasty glare. "Be like what, Colton? *Cautious?* We just crashed into nothing! I think this guy, Adu, has the right to talk about all sorts of scenarios."

Colton kept his mouth shut. Although not weak-looking by any means, he seemed like a follower more than a leader. And with the way Emma had spoken to him, I expected these two had known each other a long time. Without a word, he sighed and shook his head, allowing his wavy light brown hair to mask his eyes.

"Maybe try going slowly," I said to James. "Or around it. It's probably a log or a rock we can't see."

Adu winced and slapped two hands over his ears as if any second now, we might explode into a thousand bits.

Carefully, James pressed on his *Go* pedal again, and we began to move forward. But it only lasted seconds—at once, the rover came to a complete stop again. This time, the impact wasn't hard or sudden, but we couldn't move.

James made a sour face and pushed harder on the pedal. The rover made a loud roaring sound, followed by a high-pitched squealing that made me sick to my stomach.

Were we crushing an animal?

"What is that?" I shouted, freaking out.

"Relax," James said. "It's the tires spinning."

I tried to calm my heart. "What does that mean?"

"It means that whatever's in our way is solid enough to keep us in place while our tires spin. It won't budge, so we aren't getting past it."

Panicked voices filled the back of the rover, and I raised a hand to quiet them.

"Let's try going around," I said.

"Why don't we go back? There's nothing out here," Emma said. She frowned hard and wrinkles formed on her weak chin.

Although she wasn't wrong, something in my gut told me to keep going.

James looked sideways at me as if waiting for my permission. I nodded briefly, and he shifted the stick in the middle of the rover and started to drive backward. He spun the steering wheel a few times, readjusting the rover's direction, and drove several yards away from whatever had blocked us. Then, he turned the wheel once more and faced north again.

His jaw muscles popped as he moved forward, anticipating another crash.

Bang.

Everyone swayed forward gently.

"What the hell?" James growled. "I don't see anything."

"Me neither," I said.

He unbuckled his seatbelt and reached for the door handle.

"Wait," I said. "If you go, we all go."

I reached for my crossbow at my feet and opened the door. The others followed, holding on to their guns. The Champions, unfortunately, hadn't been assigned guns. All they held were fighting batons, which I supposed would prove useful if we were in close-range combat. But it still seemed unfair that everyone else had high-powered weapons except for them.

They clutched the sticks, moving cautiously through the weeds and wildflowers. Even if there was a large boulder, or a fallen tree, I wasn't so sure we'd see it. I couldn't even see my own feet.

"Can you hand me that?" I asked Emma, wiggling my fingers at her baton.

She handed me her weapon and I held it by the very end. With the opposite end, I poked around in the grass, trying to feel for something hard.

"Come on," I muttered, hoping to find something.

Colton, the other Champion, followed my lead and began searching the vegetation with his baton. Being that he was short and stocky—even shorter than Adu—it wasn't long before he disappeared into the vegetation. The others stood by, looking confused.

Suddenly, the end of my baton hit something hard.

"Here," I said, jabbing it at the ground again.

"What is it?" James asked.

I dragged the baton along the hard surface, trying to get an idea of its shape, but something was off.

"I-I don't know," I admitted, poking around some more.

The surface felt smooth, and flat, which meant it wasn't a rock or a log. It had to be something else. I dragged the baton horizontally, wondering how far this thing stretched. But no matter how many steps I took toward James, I couldn't get away from it.

"Give me that," James said, grabbing the baton out of Colton's hand.

Holding his new stick firmly, James moved quickly toward the mysterious object. But suddenly, he smashed into something unseen and stumbled backward, reaching for his forehead.

"What the—"

In front of me, thousands of ripples ran through the air like current in a river. They spread out and expanded circularly, moving away from where James had hit his forehead. I craned my neck, watching as these peculiar translucent ripples moved toward the sky before disappearing.

Emma scowled at the clouds. "What the hell was that?"

I stared at James, who rubbed his forehead.

I was too stunned to say anything. Instead, I raised my baton and carefully poked the spot James had walked into. Although not as prominent, more ripples trickled away from the tip of my baton. I began tapping my stick in various spots, and no matter where I touched—high up, on the side, or right in front of me—the same thing happened.

It was like a giant, invisible wall.

How was this possible?

I hit harder this time, but all it did was cause larger ripples to swim away.

"Are we trapped?" Adu asked, sounding panicked. He paced through the weeds, bits of crispy vegetation sticking to his black pants. "This doesn't make any sense. What is that? An invisible force field? Have we all died? Is this all an illusion? A false reality?"

Suddenly, James shouted and swung his baton as hard as he could at the unseen barrier.

This time, streaks of bright blue light similar to flashes of lightning flickered all around the impact area, and even larger waves danced through the air, distorting the field in front of us.

When the wall didn't budge, James started running away from us, dragging the stick against the mysterious wall. As his baton scratched the surface, a residual line formed, but it lasted only seconds before fading and becoming completely clear again.

James's voice became fainter and fainter as he ran. Eventually, he disappeared into the thick greenery, and all we could see was the tip of his baton bouncing around.

"This is ridiculous," Westin said, inspecting the wall. Carefully, he raised a stiff finger and slowly moved toward it.

I grabbed his arm. "Don't."

We didn't know what this thing was. All we knew was that it was solid enough to keep the rover out. If technology could be so advanced, maybe it had the potential to harm us, too. Maybe if we kept poking and prodding at it, something else would happen.

And I didn't want to find out what that *something* was.

"James!" I shouted.

I winced in his direction, hoping to spot his stick.

But it was gone.

"Where did he go?" I asked.

The other female fighter whose name I didn't know shrugged. "James has a temper. Give him a few minutes and he'll calm down."

Her voice was deep and calculated, and I imagined she was the most levelheaded one in the group. She hadn't spoken a word until now. Unlike Emma, who had long blond hair tied into a bun, this woman had straight, medium-length brown hair on only one side of her head. The other side was shaved entirely.

It was an odd hairdo, but it looked cool on her.

We waited for several minutes, but James didn't return.

"Maybe we should go after him," Colton said.

Emma shook her head. "And leave the rover alone?"

"Any of you know how to drive it?" I asked.

"Wouldn't matter if we did," said the woman with the partially shaved head. "James has the key."

I rolled my neck until something cracked, then sighed. "All right. Let's go find him. Keep your weapons up."

I cocked my crossbow, then kept it up as I led everyone through the green and yellow plants. Some of them scratched my knuckles and irritated my skin, so I tried to use the tip of my crossbow to clear a path.

No one spoke, and we moved one quiet step at a time. I wanted to shout James's name, but I was afraid that if he'd been captured by enemies, we'd make our presence known. If he was in trouble, it was better for us to approach without being spotted.

We walked for several minutes, and every now and then, I spotted a print in the ground. It was messy, and barely visible with all the dry yellow weeds flattened around it, but I knew it was his. The vegetation around us became so dense that I had to aggressively swipe my crossbow from side to side to clear a path.

"How far do you think he went?" Westin whispered.

No matter how discreet he tried to be, it didn't work. He was the tallest and largest of the group, and when he whispered, it was grumbly sounding and far-reaching, like the vibrations of an earthquake.

I parted my lips, prepared to say, "I don't know," when rapid footsteps rushed toward us.

Weeds shook in the distance and a hissing sound filled the air. I looked for a baton in the air, but I couldn't see one. Was it James?

I raised my crossbow, prepared to fire my bolt if necessary, when James's bright eyes appeared right in front of me. He came charging so fast that he nearly jabbed his own chest into the point of my bolt.

"Holy!" he said. "What the hell are you guys doing?"

I lowered my crossbow and frowned at him.

"Looking for you!"

His cheeks were rosy and he breathed in fast, his shoulders bouncing up and down. "I had to see how far it reached."

"And?" I asked.

Through labored breathing, he shook his head. "Keeps going. It's like there's no end. I didn't bother continuing." He leaned forward, pressing his hands on his knees, and spat next to his boots. Then, he stood up tall again, looking exhausted. "Whatever this thing is, it has us trapped from the rest of the world."

"Do you think it's all around the bunker?" Emma asked. "Or just here?"

James shrugged. "I don't know. We never go farther than a certain point when we explore. So if this thing does wrap around us farther out, we wouldn't know."

We looked at each other pensively.

"It has to end," Adu said.

"Says who?" James asked. "We don't even know what this is."

"Maybe Elias does," I said. "Maybe some people inside the bunker are from this side of the river. We should go back and talk to him about it."

No one argued. It felt like the smartest move.

With our weapons lowered, we made our way back to the rover. Everyone kept bickering about how this wall didn't make any sense, and how maybe aliens had planted it to keep humans contained. The whole idea sounded preposterous, but at this point, we couldn't discount anything.

The next thing I knew, Emma and James were arguing about what aliens would look like, if they existed. It was a pointless conversation, but I was glad the Champions and Elias's fighters were having a conversation.

When we reached the rover, I made my way back to the other side and reached for the handle. But before I could grab it, warm hands snatched me from behind. I tried to shout out, but my mouth was immediately covered, and no matter how hard I tried to fight back, it was no use.

I was pulled into the weeds, and everyone disappeared from view.

CHAPTER 16

Where is she?" Emma whispered.

I wanted to shout, "I'm here!" but I couldn't. I stood frozen in place with a warm body behind me. It felt large and strong and held me firmly in place. Something cold and sharp suddenly pressed into my neck—a wordless threat warning me that if I didn't keep quiet, they'd slit my throat.

"She disappeared in there," someone said.

The sound of shuffling surrounded us, and my attacker squeezed me even tighter, holding me firmly in place.

"No one has to get hurt," came a deep, croaky voice. "Tell your people to drop their weapons and to give me access to your wheeled machine."

Wheeled machine? What was he talking about? The rover?

He wants the keys.

From my peripheral, I caught a glimpse of

his arm—muscular, tan, and full of tribal markings. The smell of rotting teeth assaulted my nose as he breathed against my neck.

When I didn't respond, he shook me hard and pressed the knife harder into my throat, making me gulp. "Tell them."

I was afraid that if I spoke, I might lure everyone into a trap.

"They don't care what happens to me," I said.

"Lies," he growled. "I know who you are."

I swallowed hard against his blade. How did he know who I was? I'd never traveled across the river before. And even if my name spread through the lands, most people knew nothing about what I looked like.

So how did this man know?

I stared wide-eyed at the vegetation around us, trying to come up with a plan. It was only then that I realized we weren't surrounded by grass, flowers, or weeds anymore; we were surrounded by wheat.

It made my black suit stand out, but not my skin.

He shook me again, this time nudging me—threatening me to move forward. When I didn't budge, he began pushing me through the wheat. Where was he taking me? I stumbled with his strong forearm wrapped around my neck, feeling like my head might explode. My face felt swollen and round, and breathing became difficult. I clawed at his skin, but he didn't loosen his grip.

"Stop it," I wanted to shout, but I couldn't speak.

"Access, or you die," he hissed in my ear. "Five seconds."

I tapped his solid arm. "I-I-I."

"Four."

I tried to kick his shin, but I was too weak.

"Three."

I tried reaching for his eyes, but he was too tall.

"Two."

"Okay... Okay," I said.

He loosened his grip.

"I'll tell—" I swallowed hard and rubbed my neck. "I'll tell them."

I parted my lips, prepared to tell everyone to lower their guns, when a thunderous sound exploded nearby, and something warm and wet splashed all over my face.

"Silver."

"Silver!"

Someone shook me from side to side. I reached for my face, feeling slime and bits of something. Some pieces were hard, others, soft. James appeared in front of me, wiping my face with the back of his hand.

"Don't worry about that," he said.

Worry? Worry about what?

As he cleaned my face, I caught glimpses of bright red blood on his skin, along with little bits of gray matter. I blinked hard, trying to understand what had happened.

I took a step back, and my foot caught on something. Thankfully, James was quick—he caught me by the collar of my shirt and pulled me back into a standing position.

"I got him," he said, eyeballing the ground. "It's better if you don't look."

Cautiously, I looked downward to find a dead body with only part of its face remaining. It was disturbing and unsettling and made me want to vomit. Immediately I looked away, wondering if I'd ever rid my mind of that image.

"I told you not to look," James said.

He wrapped his arm around me and guided me back to the rover. "Let's go home."

I turned away, trying to make sense of it all, when I suddenly realized something. I stopped midtrack and turned around to look at the body.

"Silver—" James tried.

"The clothing," I said. "The burn marks..."

Emma and Colton stepped forward.

They knew.

"This is a Woodface," I said.

"A what?" James asked.

Ignoring him, I turned to Emma and Colton. "I thought Elias got them all."

"Maybe a few got away," Emma said.

"Or maybe they were never killed," Colton said.

I pondered that for a moment. Elias had nothing to gain by keeping our enemies alive. If anything, they were a risk to his people. But what didn't add up for me was how Elias had specifically asked that I go out scavenging knowing full well how badly the Elites wanted me. Maybe in his mind, he'd hoped something would happen, even if he hadn't intentionally planned for it.

"Or, maybe there are more of them than we know about," I said.

Emma watched me and cocked her head. "Do you really think that? Or do you think this was a setup?"

Westin leaned forward, inspecting the bloody scene. "A setup? What do you mean?"

"To get rid of me," I said coldly.

James laughed. "Why on Earth would anyone try to get rid of you?"

"Because that's what everyone wants," I said, my voice resonating a bit farther than I'd hoped. "That's why our enemies—the Woodfaces—showed up in the first place. They want *me*."

There was a moment of silence until James scoffed. "Elias wouldn't do something like that."

"How do we know?" asked the nameless female fighter.

"Sierra, come on," James said. "Elias is a good leader."

"What makes you think Elias did this?" Sierra said.

"Reina told me the order came from Elias," I said.

"Maybe she was mistaken," Sierra said. "Or—"

"Reina wouldn't betray me," I said through gritted teeth.

Sierra nodded slowly, pouting her lips. It was a condescending look that translated to, *Okay, whatever you say.*

"Why don't we all head back?" James asked. "We shouldn't be standing around in a field like this. There could be more of them."

As James spoke, I stared at the spikes of wheat swaying in the wind. It was all around us. And if this entire thing had been a setup, I needed to prove my worth—I needed to show Elias that trying to get rid of me had been a mistake.

I wiped blood away from my eyebrow. "Fill up the rover with wheat. Then we leave."

CHAPTER 17

Reina waited for us as we slowly drove back into the underground lot.

James was much more gentle about going into the bunker than he had been zooming out earlier. Carefully, he stationed the rover between two small vehicles. My heart thudded hard as I waited for Reina to scowl at the rover and point out damage, but she didn't. Before returning, we'd gone over the rover several times, and nothing seemed out of the ordinary. I still couldn't understand how there was no damage given how hard we'd crashed into that invisible wall. We'd back away without trouble, and the rover still drove perfectly.

At first, Reina looked relieved as she watched me unbuckle my seatbelt through the front window. But the moment I stepped out, her lips contorted into an upside-down smile.

"Silver!" she called out, rushing to me.

The rover might not have been damaged,

but I was.

She grabbed my face and examined it for a wound.

"I'm fine," I said, swallowing my anger.

Although I knew Reina had nothing to do with this, I wished she'd pushed back harder against Elias's order. It still didn't make sense to me that he wanted me out there. And the more I thought about it, the more I felt like he hoped I wouldn't return.

"Woodface," I said, matter-of-factly.

Her brown eyes bulged and she inspected me again as if trying to uncover answers in the blood on my face.

"What? How? Where?" she blurted.

"I want to talk to Elias," I said.

She seemed surprised by my bold demand. "Silver—"

"Now."

Sighing, she clasped her hips and bowed her head. "It's late, Silver. Everyone's gone to bed, including Elias. Why don't you get cleaned up, and we can discuss it with him in the morning?"

I wanted to storm up to his room, pound on his door, and demand that he give me answers to whatever little game he was playing. I'd almost died out there. We had almost died out there. Worse, if it weren't for James, that Woodface could have gained access to the rover and infiltrated the bunker.

My thoughts were a little unrealistic though. First, the Woodface wouldn't have known how to drive, and second, he would have had to jump the ramp again and know where the bunker was located.

Everything seemed to point to this whole situation being a fluke, but I couldn't help my anger toward Elias. If he had at least taken the time to talk to me before leaving, maybe I wouldn't be this angry. Maybe I wouldn't have felt like he was being manipulative or deceitful.

But what was eating away at me the most was not knowing who that Woodface was or how he'd found us. And how had he known who I was? Had a drawing of me circulated the lands? Was it all simply bad luck? How had he ended up on the other side of the river?

My head spun.

Maybe he'd run away during the tank attack and jumped into the water.

Or, maybe we had only defeated part of their army, and they were preparing for retaliation.

"Silver," Reina said, pulling me out of a whirlwind of thoughts. "You should get some rest."

I wasn't so sure I'd be able to sleep after the day I'd had, but Reina was right. I had to try. Despite feeling wide awake, I was exhausted.

I flinched when James patted my shoulder—a gesture meant to signify, *Well done today.*

Everyone else did the same thing, and it felt like they were thanking me. Before exiting the parking lot, James positioned his sunglasses on top of his head and threw his chin out at Reina.

"If this was a setup, you guys are a bunch of fools." He chewed on a wheat stalk, holding it by the spike. "Silver here's the first person in years to find us a real supply of food."

I parted my lips to say it was a team effort, but he winked at me and exited, the others following close behind.

Reina looked at me, confused, so I reached for the rover's back door and opened it wide, and a massive amount of wheat spilled out, forming a pile at her feet.

When morning arrived, I wasn't certain I'd slept.

I'd spent most of the night tossing and turning, reliving the prior day's attack. If it weren't for James, I wouldn't have returned. I got dressed in one of the clean uniforms Alvan had given me—a navy blue outfit that was both comfortable and surprisingly nice. Until I figured out how to get regular civilian clothes,

176

I settled for this.

By the time I got to the dining hall, it was mostly empty. A few parents remained, urging their children to finish their breakfasts before school.

"Silver!" Arahm called out, his voice reverberating off the wooden walls.

I made my way over to him near the back bar, to where he and his children stood proudly, prepared to serve me anything I asked for.

"Thanks to you, we'll have pancakes tomorrow," he said, beaming.

I must have crinkled my nose.

"Word spreads fast around here." He raised a brow. "Eggs?"

I nodded. "Yes, please."

He scooped up a ladle full of bright yellow eggs and dropped them onto a white ceramic plate. Next to him, his daughter—a little girl with big brown eyes and thick brows like her father—hopped up and down on her tippytoes, pointing at a large dish with only a few pieces of cantaloupe remaining.

"Fruit?" she asked.

I smiled. "Yes, please."

I thanked them for my food and ate in silence. Now and then, people walked by and nodded courteously my way. It was a drastic change compared to only a few days ago, when most Undergrounders had given me menacing looks that told me they wanted nothing to do with me or our people.

But now, all I felt was gratitude.

Was this about the wheat? Was that what Arahm had meant when he said we'd be getting to eat pancakes? I finished my meal, thanked him again, and stepped out into the courtyard.

But it looked nothing like the courtyard I'd seen only days ago.

Now, wooden targets hung on the sidewall at the far back, where archers sat in the grass, carving bows. Closer to the entrance, several dozen Champions fought with batons, practicing their moves. Others sat on boulders or benches, using knives to carve out weapons.

About halfway through the courtyard, I spotted Dax, along with several other men, working on what appeared to be a wooden barrier wall separating these new fighting grounds from the rest of the people.

"Careful!" Dax shouted, ordering the men to raise a large piece of wood into the air. The fence wasn't finished, but they'd done most of the work, and it was wide enough to allow archers to practice their aim without the risk of harming anyone in the garden beds.

I spotted Sadie and she came jogging toward me. She looked better today and in less pain. Still, she probably wouldn't be using any weapons for several more weeks.

"Isn't this great?" she asked, planting her hands on her hips.

I couldn't believe how drastically different the courtyard looked—all within one day.

"When did this happen?" I asked, admiring the new layout.

"Yesterday," she said. "Elias made an announcement. He said that after giving it some thought, he decided we can train part-time, so long as we keep helping around when needed."

"Didn't that cause trouble?" I asked.

Just the other day, the Undergrounders made it obvious that they were getting tired of hearing the Champions complain about wanting to train. Now, we'd taken up half their courtyard.

Why weren't they upset about it?

"Yeah, at first," she admitted. "They weren't happy about it, just like we weren't happy about having to work construction or do garden work. But we do what we have to do."

As I watched everyone going about their daily chores, I couldn't help but notice that there wasn't any hostility. At least, none that I could see. Everyone worked quietly, some people laughing, others playfully nudging one another. Both the Undergrounders and the people of Ortus seemed to be getting along just fine.

"What changed?" I asked.

Sadie looked at me like I was a complete moron. "What changed? Are you kidding? A few days ago, these people thought they were going to starve because of us. And now, you show up with a bunch of wheat." She smacked my shoulder. "You saved us."

CHAPTER 18

Although thankful for having made a difference in the bunker, I needed more answers, and Elias was the only person who could give them to me.

"Silver, where—" Sadie tried, but I quickly left the courtyard.

People smiled at me as I walked past them, and I did my best to return their polite gestures. But my mind was racing. It was hard to look up and acknowledge people when all I could do was keep replaying yesterday's events—the wall... the Woodface.

"Hey," came a familiar voice.

James stood in front of me without his sunglasses. He reminded me a bit of Lyson with his light features, only less baby-faced and shorter. That was where the similarities ended. James seemed like the kind of guy who liked to get in trouble if it meant he got to have some fun. He'd proven this to me when I'd first met him by speeding out of the parking lot and sending us flying through the air.

It had been rude, aggressive, and completely uncalled for.

But I owed him everything. He'd saved my life.

"Have you talked to Elias yet?" he asked. "The gang's been wondering about it. And listen, we only told people about the wheat, not about—"

I nodded as a way of telling him to stop talking. I was thankful he hadn't brought up the invisible wall to anyone else. If he had, it would have only stirred panic.

"I'm looking for him now," I said. "I need to talk to him—"

"Well, well, well," came Jared's obnoxious voice.

He strolled into the central hub, his heavy boots smacking against the tiled floor. As he walked, he slid his finger across one of the bright red sofa chairs. Behind him were a handful of men—the same men who had been with him in the shooting range a few days prior.

"The team who saved the day," Jared said, sneering at me.

I hated his twisted smile. It looked evil in every sense and made him look like he was plotting awful things in his mind and getting a kick out of it.

"What do you want, Jared?" James asked.

He puffed out his chest and stepped in front of me. I wasn't sure if he'd done it on purpose, or if the thought of defending me had been subconscious. Either way, I didn't need to be defended. I stepped sideways to get a clear view of Jared.

"I just wanted to extend my congratulations on the successful scavenge," Jared said. He turned to his broad-shouldered men. "Isn't that right, boys?"

Today especially, Jared looked more sickly than usual. He was already pale to begin with, but under his eyes were dark bags that made me wonder if he'd spent the entire night tossing and turning. His cheeks were sunken, making him look like a vampire, and the only color in his face came from the scruff of his beard growing in—a dark brown. Even then, it was so dark it looked black like the rest of his hair.

Jared's men laughed.

What was so funny?

"Have you seen Elias?" I asked.

Jared's sneer returned. "My brother? He spends most of his days studying in his room rather than being with his people."

His words came out with resentment.

"Where's his room?" I asked.

Jared inspected me from head to toe as if assessing whether or not I was worthy of receiving such information.

"B24," he said. "But you don't have access to the subbasement floor."

I was surprised to learn that Elias spent his days so far underground. I had expected his room to be somewhere higher, closer to his people. But maybe he enjoyed the silence.

Jared stared at me. What was he thinking? The man was impossible to read. It was like he enjoyed toying with me.

"Then how do I get down there?" I asked.

He tucked his thumbs into his leather belt. "Well, me and my boys could bring you—"

"I have access," came Reina's voice.

She marched toward us with her shoulders drawn back. She gave Jared a nasty glare that made me thankful I wasn't on her bad side.

"Well, if it isn't hero lady," Jared said.

I expected him to smile, but instead, his lips curved downward like he'd eaten a rotten apple.

"Aren't you the leader's brother?" Reina asked. Despite having to tilt her head back to look at him, she spoke to him as if he were nothing but a child.

Jared's sour face contorted even more.

"If you think walking around bullying people is going to earn you Elias's position in this bunker, think again," Reina said. "Grow up. If you want people to listen to you, start being nice for a change."

He weighed her words carefully, possibly trying to decide between threatening her and apologizing for being such an *asshole*, as Grandma would say.

His gaze shifted onto me, then James, and he slowly bowed his head. "Let me know if you have any trouble accessing the basement."

It didn't sound menacing this time. Maybe he'd meant it.

Without thanking him, Reina grabbed my arm and gently pulled me away from him. We walked through one of the hallways, all the way to the back door. I wasn't sure where we were going, but it looked like Reina was familiar with the place. When I turned back, James was gone.

He must have felt out of place with Reina around.

"Elias is waiting for you," she said, slowing her pace. "He and Finn are talking now."

I followed quietly as we descended a set of concrete stairs. When we stepped into the subbasement, I was surprised to find that it wasn't as vast as the floor above us. Everything here felt crammed and narrow. We'd barely walked down the corridor when Reina stopped in front of a wooden door and knocked on it.

It creaked open, and Finn's face popped

into view.

"Come on in," he said, opening the door wider.

Elias's room was large and dimly lit, with a few lamps standing on wooden tables throughout. I was taken aback by a dancing flame atop a wax candle, but when Finn caught me staring at it, he said, "It isn't real."

Not real? How could fire not be real? I approached it cautiously, then swept my hand over the flame. It didn't dance in the slightest, nor was it warm. Slowly, I lowered my palm over it and jumped back when the flame poked my skin.

Finn laughed and grabbed it. He played with the tip, then showed me his unburned fingers. "See? It's not actually fire. It's decorative."

Elias laughed in the background. I spun around to find him sitting on a brown sofa with his legs crossed and one arm resting on the back cushion. "Fire isn't allowed in the bunker. It's too big of a risk."

I stared in awe as Finn put it back on the desk.

The furniture in here looked old yet well taken care of. Even the lamps appeared centuries old, with their golden finishes and uniquely shaped bulbs.

Overhead, black and copper pipes ran in

various directions, most of these covered in cobwebs. There was no fancy ceiling, yet it suited the room's overall decor.

Most walls were made of concrete, except for the back wall that looked like it was built of old gray brick. In the middle of it stood a tall fireplace mantle, and under it, bright red flames danced from side to side. Beneath the flames were large crystal rocks that reflected an orange glow.

I blinked hard. "Is *that* fake, too?"

Elias smiled. "Sure is. Found this bad boy a few miles from here. It's an electric fireplace. Just an illusion." He reached for something next to the sofa and pressed a button. At once, the flames changed to a bright purple and I gasped.

How was that even possible? I'd never seen anything so beautiful.

Elias seemed amused by my reaction.

I was so impressed with the uniqueness of his room that I'd completely forgotten why I had come here in the first place—to scold him and to demand answers.

But then, I spotted books. They sat messily atop an oval-shaped table near Elias's feet.

I couldn't believe what I was seeing. Hardbacks—with covers indicating a variety of subjects:

Plumbing

Electricity

Architecture

Gardening and Harvesting

"You're studying all of this?" I asked.

Elias nodded. "I have to. If I expect the people around here to follow me, I need to be the most knowledgeable man here."

I admired his way of thinking. While Jared thought spending time with his people was the better approach, Elias sought knowledge to better the lives of those around him.

But as he sat there, smiling with little moon-shaped eyes, I thought back to yesterday, and how we'd run into the invisible wall. Then, I thought of the Woodface, and I clenched my fists.

"Did you know?" I asked.

He breathed out through his nose. "Yes."

My heart skipped a beat. How had he admitted it so easily? I took a step forward, teeth clenched, but Reina stopped me.

I opened my mouth, prepared to lash out at him, when he added, "My father discovered it years ago. He blew up the bridge to discourage others from feeling the same overwhelming defeat he felt. We don't know where it comes from. And most of my people don't know about it, either. So I ask that you keep this between us."

What was he talking about? Had I missed

something?

Then, my eyes bulged. While I'd been thinking about the Woodface, Elias had been talking about the wall.

He knew about it!

"You were never meant to go over the river, Silver," he said. A playful smile tugged at his lips. "How on Earth did you pull that off, by the way? Our people have been discouraged time and again from going beyond the river."

I wasn't sure whether to tell him about the ramp. If I did, maybe he'd destroy it. So instead, I kept my mouth shut. He seemed to understand that I didn't want to tell him. Uncrossing his legs, he reached for a mug of something next to his books and took a sip.

"You seem angry, Silver. I'm sorry you had to find the wall—"

"This isn't about the wall," I said coldly. "I was attacked."

He nearly spat his drink back out into his mug. The scowl on his face told me he knew nothing about it. "Attacked? By who?"

"A Woodface," I said.

Finn and Reina frowned at the same time, likely confused. And why wouldn't they be? Elias had promised to take out the Woodface army. Had he lied? Had he failed?

"I-I don't know what to say," Elias said. "I placed the order. The tank went out, and shots were fired. I verified our projectile stock myself the moment the tank returned."

Then, something hit me.

"Did Jared go out?" I asked.

Elias placed his mug back down. "What do you mean?"

"Was he the one to lead the tank?"

Elias bowed his head like he knew what I was getting at. "No. I love my brother—I do. But I'm not an idiot. I know he has his own intentions and can't always be trusted. I assure you, he wasn't in that tank. I made sure of it myself."

I was relieved to hear this. At least now I knew that Jared hadn't gone out and sabotaged the attack.

"Maybe a few escaped," Reina said. "Why else would that Woodface have been on the other side of the river? Was there only one?"

I nodded. "As far as I know."

"Then let's not jump to conclusions," Elias said. "I'm happy to send a few troops out to explore if you'd like. If any of them are lingering nearby, we'll take care of it."

I was thankful for his cooperation and willingness to take care of the matter. But what I didn't understand was how neither Finn nor Reina had reacted to the news about the wall.

"Did you know, too?" I asked. "About the wall?"

Finn looked sad. "Elias told us this morning."

"Then where does it come from?" I asked.

Slowly, Elias stood up in front of the purple fireplace and stretched his back. "We don't know. Neither did my father. Before we found the bunker, we explored these lands for days. The wall seems to form a rectangle around us. My father never located the other walls, but the information was given to him by travelers."

I thought back to the men with guns who had attacked our people a few weeks prior. Did this mean they were in our vicinity? Were they also trapped within these walls? If so, it meant we were at risk of running into them while scavenging. Or, was the rectangle *that* big? And why was it there at all?

"Do you think this is Elite technology?" I asked.

Elias looked dumbfounded. "Your guess is as good as mine."

Closing my eyes, I sighed. I thought the days of being confined were behind me, and now, I'd discovered that we were once again trapped between walls. I wasn't sure whether to feel angry or heartbroken.

"Don't give those walls too much thought," Elias said. "They've never stopped us before. We've traveled for miles in the opposite direction, and there is still plenty to scavenge."

"What happens when we run out of places to explore?" I asked.

Elias looked puzzled by my question. "Life isn't only about exploring, Silver. It's about building. We go out to gather resources now and then, but what matters is what we do inside our walls. Our crops. Our livestock. Our people."

Although comforted by his words, there was one last question I was dying to ask him. With how honest he'd been from the moment I entered the room, I felt confident he wouldn't try to hide anything from me.

"Why did you send me out there?" I asked. "I'm not the best fighter. I'm not a leader. And I'm wanted by the Elites."

"Silver—" Reina tried.

"No," I said sharply. "I want to know. Did you want me killed? Captured?"

Elias pulled his face back as if I'd thrown his mug at him. Then, his thick brows descended and a prominent frown formed lumps on his forehead. "Why would I do something like that?"

"I don't know," I said. "That's why I'm asking. Because it doesn't make any sense to me."

"You did what I was hoping you'd do, Silver," he said, matter-of-factly. "You led a successful search and brought food back for all of us. Your reputation is well known around here. I couldn't very well have you sit back while our people supplied your people with basic necessities. It was causing resentment. My people started to blame your people for inevitable food shortages. Now, the Girl Who Refused Immortality eliminated everyone's worries in a single day."

"But, it could have been anyone else—"

"No," he cut me off. "It had to be *you*. Your people were willing to die for you, Silver. They'll follow you wherever you go. So I sent you out there to prove your worth. I had no idea you would be attacked, and for that, I'm truly sorry. But if we want any chance at taking down the Elites, we need my people on board. We need them to follow you, too."

"How did you know I'd succeed?" I asked.

He paused, rubbed his chin in amusement, and said, "A gut feeling."

CHAPTER 19

Sadie leaned forward, resting her elbows next to her plate of vegetables and rice. "You're going out *again?*"

She sounded annoyed by it, like I'd just told her I had to pee for the fifth time in the last hour.

Dax sat down with two plates, and her new friend—or girlfriend, I wasn't sure—sat down next to her.

"Everyone, this is Mia," she said.

Mia smiled a beautiful set of glossy white teeth that looked like snow in contrast to her light brown complexion. She had symmetrical features, sparkling brown eyes, and a long dark braid that started at the top of her head and hung over one shoulder. Unlike Dax, who wore torn clothing covered with dirt and grass stains, Mia wore a clean white blouse coupled with silky blank pants.

"I only have a few minutes," Mia said. "I'm

on shift tonight."

Dax inclined her head toward Mia. "The bar."

Everyone around our table gave Mia a welcoming smile and a nod. I was thankful to see that our groups were beginning to merge.

I leaned into Sadie, our noses nearly touching. "And *that's* why I'm going out."

She scrunched her nose, glanced sideways at Mia, and sat up straight. "Are you attracted to M—"

"What? No," I exclaimed. "I'm talking about uniting our people."

Sadie scoffed. "You act like it's *your* responsibility to unite everyone. Like these are your people."

I placed my fork down and stared at her cold in the face. "It is my responsibility. I almost got all of you killed, and I'm the one who led you inside this place."

Sadie went quiet, gently scraping the tip of her fork on her plate. She moved her vegetables around but didn't eat.

"What do you care?" I asked.

Was she jealous that I was taking on more responsibility? What was her problem?

Her icy blue eyes narrowed on me, and I wondered if maybe I was crossing a line with my attitude.

"What do I care?" she repeated.

Everyone around us stopped eating to watch the scene unfold.

"I have a heart, Silver, despite what you may think. And I don't want you going out there and dying."

She dropped her fork onto her plate with a loud clang and stormed off.

I blinked hard, trying to understand what had just happened. Was this whole thing about her being worried? I hadn't even told her about the Woodface, or about the wall. Now, I was thankful I'd kept my mouth shut.

Maybe it was better to keep those details private.

"You gonna chase after her? Or..." Dax said.

I flattened my eyelids as a way of telling her to mind her own business. She raised two hands in submission and said, "All right, all right, but if it was me—"

"She needs space," I said, jabbing my fork into a little pile of rice. "I'll talk to her after."

Next to Dax, Rose made a hand gesture I didn't understand. Danika watched her, smiled, then said, "She says Sadie cares about you and that you shouldn't be annoyed about that."

I forced a smile at Rose. I knew she meant well. She was one of the sweetest people I'd ever met and all she wanted was for everyone to get along.

But as thankful as I was to have someone

care about me like that, I didn't appreciate the anger I was receiving. It wasn't like I had a choice in the matter. Elias had specifically asked me to go out again with the same scavenging crew. Who was I to say no? I didn't want Sadie to be upset with me for doing something good.

In a sense, her anger made me feel trapped, and I hated that feeling more than anything.

I finished supper without another word and returned to my room. As my door swept open, Sadie stepped out of hers.

"Hey," she said, looking ashamed.

I stared at her. "Hey."

"Got a minute?" she asked.

I didn't say anything, and she followed me into my room.

Neither of us spoke as we removed our shoes and made our way to the bed. I sat on the edge, and Sadie sat next to me, her fingers intertwined together over her knees.

"Look, I'm sorry," she said without looking up. "If I were going out there with you, I wouldn't be this worked up."

"You're injured," I said. "You can't—"

"I know that, Silver. I'm saying *if* I were able to go with you. I don't like the idea of you being out there without me."

I paused, waiting to see if she had more to say. When she stayed quiet, I said, "I understand, but I'm in good hands, I promise."

I felt awful for not telling her about the Woodface. It felt like I was lying to her. But what good would it serve? If she knew about it, she'd spend her entire day worrying about me getting attacked again.

"They have guns," I said.

She rolled her eyes until they landed on me. "I know that. I'm not an idiot. I know you're well protected out there. But there's always a risk, especially when it comes to you."

She wasn't wrong. If the Elites knew where I was, there was no telling how far they'd go to get a hold of me. For all I knew, we could run into an army tomorrow. It was a huge risk. But if I hadn't taken a risk to begin with—like agreeing to go over that river—we wouldn't have found all that wheat.

Risks were a necessary part of life.

Staring at her locked fingers, she said, "Promise me you'll be safe."

I'd never seen this side of Sadie before. She was always criticizing me or finding ways to make me feel small. But now, it was obvious that my leaving the bunker was eating away at her. I wondered if maybe this was the side of her she'd fought so hard to hide from me.

"I promise," I said.

Her sad blue eyes rolled up at me and locked into position. It made me feel awkward.

I couldn't tell what she was thinking, but whatever it was, it turned my stomach upside down.

Then, without a word, she leaned forward and gently pressed her lips on mine. They felt warm and silky, and unlike anything I'd ever felt before. My eyes involuntarily shut as I breathed in her scent—a mixture of soap, grass, and flowers. Everything around me faded, and I wished this moment would last forever.

My stomach sank and danced at the same time, and when she pulled away, the room around me seemed to reappear in a rapid swirl as if by magic—as if everything around me had been suctioned away during that kiss.

She rubbed my cheek with her thumb and said, "For good luck."

The next morning, I entered the parking lot with a smile.

"You excited to get more wheat?" James teased.

I wiped the goofy smile off my face and cleared my throat. I hadn't realized I'd been smiling all morning. But how could I not? That kiss... it was exactly as Grandma had described. She'd said that when I experienced my first kiss, it would either be gross and cold, or warm and magical, depending on the person. She'd also told me if it was with the right person, it would be the latter.

Did this mean that Sadie was the right person for me?

My stomach did flips again and I caught James staring at me above the frames of his sunglasses.

"Someone had a good night," Sierra said without smiling. She loaded her gun into the back of the rover.

Her tone sounded suggestive, yet I wasn't even sure what she was implying.

"Leave the girl alone," Colton said. He shook his curly brown hair away from his eyes and placed his fighting baton against Sierra's gun.

"You ready to go again?" James asked.

In truth, I was both excited and terrified to go back out there. My heart pounded at the thought of being attacked again, and the more I thought about it, the more I flashed back to the Woodface grabbing me from behind. I'd felt his heartbeat against my back, his hot breath against my neck, and his sharp cold blade against my throat.

But then, I thought of Sadie's soft lips on mine, and my fear melted away.

I'd be okay—I had to be if I ever wanted to feel *that* again.

I hopped into the right side of the vehicle, with James at the wheel. He lowered the windows and Reina wished us good luck. When he pressed the big blue button at the center of the console, the bunker's massive door opened.

"See you in a bit," he said to Reina.

She smacked the hood of the rover and walked away.

James looked at me like a kid asking their parents for a second serving of food.

It made me smile. I knew what he wanted.

"Go ahead," I said.

With that, he slammed the Go pedal and the wheels squealed in the parking lot before we took off, speeding up the ramp. In my side mirror, Reina grabbed her forehead and shook her head, without a doubt disapproving of James's aggressive driving habits.

In a moment, we were in the air again.

It lasted only seconds, but it reminded me of my first kiss—a floating, gut-twisting feeling that made me feel on top of the world.

When we landed, my head snapped forward and I was yanked back to reality.

"Want some music?" James asked.

"Music?" I repeated, confused. "What do you mean?"

Grinning, he reached for a dial and music started playing inside the rover.

I couldn't believe it. Where was it coming

from? I slid my hand across the dashboard, trying to locate its source, then swung around to see how the other Champions were reacting. Like me, they were impressed.

So we drove for hours—over the ramp and toward the endless wheat field—listening to all sorts of music.

CHAPTER 20

As time passed, our crew left the bunker every other day to gather more wheat. On my off days, I spent my time in the courtyard, training with the others. Bit by bit, we created new weapons to replace those we'd lost to the tornado.

Every time we went back out, James introduced me to new music. He seemed to have an endless supply of it, and it blew my mind. He'd put something on, then explain the genre and the history.

"You love music," I said, watching him.

Nodding to the melodic tune coming out through the rover's speakers, he didn't say a word and bobbed his head to the rhythm.

The day of our seventh outing, I entered the parking lot in the early morning as I'd done the last five times. This time, however, Reina wasn't there to wish us good luck, likely because her confidence in us had grown. We gathered our weapons and loaded up the rover while James verified the vehicle's charge gauge.

He did this every time we went out. Apparently, one time, they hadn't checked the gauge and it hadn't properly charged overnight. The rover got stuck a few miles from here, and they had to call in to get the rover towed back.

"All set?" James asked, leaning against his open door.

Everyone nodded and climbed inside.

But before I got in, the sound of a door blasting open pulled my attention to the back of the room.

In came Jared with three other men behind him.

"You weren't planning on leaving without me, were you?" he asked.

I glanced at James through the rover's interior. Did he know anything about this? The puzzled look on his face told me he had no idea what was going on. The others, who were now sitting in the back, twisted their necks to look at Jared through the tinted windows.

What's going on? Emma mouthed.

I shrugged and made a face that translated to, *I have no idea.*

"This is our mission," James said. "We already have Elias's approval to go out."

"And we're here to help you get some wheat," Jared said. "Save you some time."

I found that hard to believe. Did he have Elias's approval to go out? Did he even need it? I knew that if I asked that question, or even tried to argue with him, things would get ugly fast. The last few encounters with Jared proved to me that he was *always* looking for trouble.

He made his way over to a row of two-wheeled vehicles with huge wheels and forest-green frames. I only knew what they were because James had told me before our last mission.

Motorcycles, often referred to simply as *bikes*.

According to James, these weren't standard built. He'd seen a real motorcycle while scavenging one time, and they were far sleeker and thinner than these. These military bikes were shaped in a way that the tires were almost as wide as the frame, and so big that the tops of them reached Jared's thighs.

I stared at the bike's bulky, heavy-looking frame as Jared searched for the right set of keys dangling from a board on the wall. He ran his finger along various numbers, then plucked four different keys from little nails.

One by one, he tossed them to his men.

"Why are you all just staring at us?" Jared asked. "Go on. Do your thing. We won't be far behind."

Reluctantly, James got inside the rover and I followed, landing hard in my seat.

"I don't trust him," I grumbled.

James started the rover, and it rumbled gently under my butt. "Me neither, but he's basically second-in-command. Not much I can do. Jared always goes out."

Biting my tongue, I watched Jared through my side mirror as he climbed onto his bike, kicked something at the back, and started moving forward. Facing us, he waited, smiling.

It was a thin-lipped smile that made me want to punch him in the face. It was forced and incredibly annoying. He reached into one of his chest pockets and extracted a pair of sunglasses. Sliding them on, he mouthed something to his men, and one by one, they rolled up beside him.

James glared at them through his rearview mirror, his grip tightening around his steering wheel. I wasn't sure why he hated Jared so much, aside from the fact that Jared was simply hateable. Maybe something had happened between the two of them that I was unaware of.

"We should go," I said.

James's white-knuckled grip loosened and he pressed the Go pedal just as the door ahead began to rise. Part of me wished Reina had been there, but I wondered if maybe that was precisely why Jared had chosen today of all days to join us in the wastelands.

He knew Reina would have put up a fight.

James didn't zoom out of the parking lot this time. He drove out slowly, his head moving up every few seconds to watch Jared behind us.

"Maybe we should go somewhere else," James said.

Westin leaned forward. "Why? Jared knows about the wheat. He wants us to take him there."

"Yeah, but why?" James asked. "Jared isn't the kind of guy who follows. And he definitely isn't the kind of guy to do grunt work."

"Maybe he wants to see how you cross the river," Sierra said, unbothered.

Everyone looked back at her.

"Makes sense," Emma said beside her. "More to explore on the other side."

"Or," Adu cut in, "maybe he simply wants to help us cut more wheat, like he said. Why do you always assume—"

Without warning, James cranked up the music, and Adu kept talking, his lips flapping as the music overpowered his voice. When he realized what was happening, he gave James the stink eye, crossed his arms, and leaned back in his seat.

I smiled, though it didn't last long. As soon

as I glanced into my side mirror again, I spotted Jared zooming along with us, tilting his bike from side to side as he drove, almost as if trying to taunt me. He'd speed up close to the rear of the rover, laugh, then slow down, and his men went on to do the same thing. It was like they were encouraging us to go faster.

There was no telling what Jared's true intentions were, but I had a bad feeling in my gut—a feeling that told me if we weren't careful out here, things could get ugly, and fast.

CHAPTER 21

The jump over the river wasn't as exciting as every other time.

I was too preoccupied watching Jared and his men through my side mirror. One by one, they jumped over the ramp we'd built and landed with a bounce on our side. They laughed and cheered, pumping their fists in the air.

Jared suddenly sped up on James's side and waved his arm, shouting something.

James slowed down to a complete stop and rolled down his window.

"Where's the field?" Jared asked.

"About three hundred miles north from here," James said. "Straight ahead."

Jared nodded abruptly as if thanking him for the information. "We'll catch up with you. Just have to check something out."

He kicked at his bike again and took off to the left, zipping through the open field.

His men followed, and a soft, rumbly sound filled the air around us.

"Do you believe that?" I asked.

James scoffed at me. "Of course not. Those bikes' energy stores can hold up to four hundred miles. They wouldn't make it to us and back, and Jared knows that."

"Like I said," Sierra cut in, "he only wanted the ramp."

"You think Elias knows about this?" I asked.

James sighed. "Does it matter? Let's do what we came here to do."

I paused, pondering this for a moment. Why would Jared have lied about his reason for following us? Why hadn't he simply been upfront about wanting to use the ramp to explore the wastelands even farther? Something wasn't adding up.

"Let's follow them," I said.

James's jaw fell open. "Why would we do that? If they want to get into trouble, that's on them."

"Aren't you curious?" I asked.

No one responded until finally, Emma said, "They'll see us coming miles away. We're in an open field."

"And we know in which direction they're going," I said. "We can wait a bit, then drive out that way. Plus, look." I pointed at thick lines of flattened grass left by their tires.

I wasn't sure why I was so keen on following Jared. Maybe it was a bad idea. James had a point—we'd come here for one reason—to gather wheat—and maybe it was best to stick to our plan.

But something told me Jared was up to no good. He couldn't very well be exposed unless we caught him in the act. The man was dangerous, and although Elias constantly defended him, it was apparent that Jared wouldn't pass an opportunity to take Elias's place. Part of me even wondered if he'd harm his own brother if it meant earning a position of power.

"No one's being forced into this," I said. "So let's vote."

Adu was the first to raise a finger. "I think this is a very bad idea. We should continue to the wheat field—"

"I'm in," Emma said. "I don't trust that guy."

"Me neither," Colton said. "Count me in."

I smiled at James who raised his sunglasses and made an effort to make eye contact with everyone in the back. It was almost as if he wanted to make sure they actually wanted this.

"Whatever you guys want," Westin said. Despite being so tall that his posture was bent sideways, he looked unbothered and leaned his head against the window.

Sierra pouted her lips and shrugged—a

gesture that I knew meant *Hell, let's do this.*

"The people have spoken," James said. He shifted his stick and started moving in the same direction as Jared and his men.

We drove incredibly slow, following their tire tracks in the grass.

James didn't put music on this time. Instead, we drove in silence and stared ahead, eyes darting in every direction. Everyone was on high alert—not only because we were tracking Jared, but also because we didn't know these lands. Threats could be looming nearby.

"We can't go too far," James said, breaking the silence. "If we return without wheat, we might have our traveling privileges revoked."

I wanted to assure him that we wouldn't follow Jared too far, but the truth was that I didn't want to stop. I needed to know what he was up to.

We drove for quite a ways, and every few minutes, James looked at me, likely wondering when I'd give the order to turn around.

"Not yet," I said.

I had a feeling we were close.

When it began to feel like a pointless mission, I caught a glimpse of something in the distance. It was small and pointed and too far to be distinguishable.

"Do you see it?" I asked, pointing at the

little black dot on the horizon.

James nodded. "Yeah. Probably a house."

"A house?" I said. "In the middle of nowhere?"

James looked amused at my comment. "Some people chose to live in seclusion before the war. It was called country living."

"Without anyone else around?" I asked.

His smirk transformed into a full-blown grin. "You're funny, Silver. Has anyone ever told you that?"

"Because there's a lot I don't know?" I asked.

I wasn't sure if he'd meant it as a joke or an insult.

At last, he responded. "Exactly. You ask the most ridiculous questions. It's entertaining. It's like talking to a five-year-old."

Emma leaned forward, frowning at him. "It's not her fault—"

But I laughed. "No, he's right. I might as well have grown up in a hole or on another planet."

Everyone in the rover laughed, and for a moment, I forgot we were following Jared. Eventually, the little black dot on the horizon turned sky blue and began to take form. It was a tall, two-story home, as James called it, and seemed to have many windows.

Next to the house was a dirt path that seemed reasonably clean and well-groomed.

Did that mean people lived here? Aside from big wooden panels covering up the windows, the place looked well-maintained. Surely someone lived inside this house.

On the dirt path were tire marks, and in front of the house, stood Jared's and his men's bikes.

What were they doing there? Did Jared know these people?

"Pull over," I said.

James looked at me curiously. "What do you mean? I thought we were going to see what they were up to."

"We are," I said. "But not in this thing. They'll see us coming."

James did as I ordered and drove the rover into an array of weeds and flowers growing in the field. They were tall and would do a good job keeping us hidden.

"Grab your weapons," I said.

Everyone looked at each other as if I'd asked them to get out and walk back to the bunker.

"You want us to point a weapon at our own people?" Sierra raised her brows.

"No," I said. "I want you to be protected in case things get bad. We have no idea who lives in that house. For all we know, Jared and his men might need our help."

Everyone did as instructed, grabbing their

guns from the back. I held on to my crossbow and stepped out, swatting a huge fly away from my face. There seemed to be even more around here. Maybe these people had farmland or livestock and attracted more insects.

We walked through the vegetation with our backs rounded, trying to blend into the greenery. Without a word, everyone followed my lead.

As we came closer to the blue house, voices seeped through the windows, or at least, what had once been windows. Only one remained intact with glass reflecting the morning sun, while the others were broken into pieces and covered with slabs of wood. I wondered if maybe the tornado had torn through this way and damaged the house. The rest of the house appeared undamaged, though it was aged and worn out, with mold climbing up the side walls. One tree sat close to the home, its leaves and branches rubbing against the rooftop.

As I stared at the old house, I bumped into something.

For a moment, I feared it might be another trick—some invisible barrier unseen to the eye.

But it was perfectly visible. Mixed in with weeds and leafy vines was a short white fence with pointed tips. I followed its tips, which appeared to make their way down to a barn, or stable.

James didn't seem bothered by it. Kicking a leg up, he climbed right over, then hopped to land on the other side.

One by one, he helped everyone climb over, except for Sierra, who refused his hand.

Once on the other side, we moved to the side of the house. But as we approached, voices slipped out through the broken windows and I held my breath.

I didn't recognize these voices, but they seemed to be pleading.

"You don't have to do this," one man said. "Please, take whatever you want."

Everyone stared at me, likely wondering what I was planning to do next.

I pointed my nose at the house and quietly rushed toward it. Pressing my back against the cool paneling, I listened.

"What do you want from us?" came another voice.

This one had belonged to a woman. She sounded frightened and on edge.

But no matter how often they pleaded or begged, no one responded to them. I looked at James and pointed at the window. I wanted to try to peek through a crack. Somehow, he understood my wordless request.

Locking his fingers together, he formed a flat surface with his palms, and I stepped onto it. The others helped keep me stable as James lifted me in the air.

With my knees bent, I slowly elevated myself until I found a crack my eye could see through. It wasn't very big, but it was enough to see a portion of the interior.

Inside was a man in a chair, his wrists bound behind his back. I shifted over slightly and spotted a woman, around the same age, sitting a bit farther away.

"Mommy," came a squeaky voice.

The woman forced a smile, though it was obvious all she wanted to do was cry.

"It's okay, sweetheart," she said.

I shifted again, this time, spotting a teenage boy glaring straight ahead like he wanted to hurt someone. But he didn't say a word. He sat there, clenching his fists behind his back. Although he didn't look old, he was surprisingly well built.

Next to him was a pair of shoes that seemed to belong to another teenager. But I couldn't see that far. So I returned my focus to the man who seemed to be doing most of the talking.

"We have food," he said. "Water. Clothes. Take it. All of it."

"I don't want that," came Jared's voice.

My heart nearly climbed into my throat. Although I knew Jared and his men were inside, part of me had hoped he wasn't the one responsible for this.

"There is something I want," Jared said.

"Anything," the man responded. "Just don't hurt my family. Please."

In the distance, a dog barked. It was a loud, deep bark that made the creature sound huge.

"Would you shut that thing up?" Jared growled.

One of his men stomped into another room and the dog growled and yelped.

"No, please!" someone cried. "Leave him alone!"

It was a girl's voice.

"Would you relax?" Jared said. "No one's hurting the dog. Pipes is just putting him outside."

He then laughed as if amused by how scared everyone had become.

A door squeaked open nearby, and I bent my knees, prepared to jump down and hide. Then, the dog growled furiously again and the door closed. It barked again, almost as if yelling at Pipes for having thrown him outside. The sound seemed to be coming from the back.

I hoped the dog was tied up, otherwise, it might find its way to the side of the house and give away our location.

I glanced down at James whose face had turned beet red. But he seemed to want to hold on. Despite his arms trembling, he nodded at me as if to say, "Keep looking."

So I returned to the window and watched as Jared stepped into my line of sight. At the same time, Pipes appeared in the background with blood dripping from his hand. He held on to it tightly, wincing.

"Bastard bit me," he grumbled.

Jared didn't seem to care. He ignored him, then smiled at the family and waved his gun in every direction.

"You see, this doesn't have to be difficult." He aimed his gun at the woman and everyone started screaming.

"Please, don't!"

"No!"

My heart thudded hard and adrenaline coursed through me. I couldn't handle it anymore.

I jumped out of James's palms, landing hard in the grass. I bent down, snatched my crossbow, and ran toward the front of the house.

"Silver!" James hissed.

I didn't listen.

Footsteps followed me as I ran up white stairs that creaked with every step. When I tore the front door open, it creaked just as loudly, and I stepped inside a house decorated mostly with wood and old furniture that sat haphazardly as if someone had pushed everything aside on purpose.

Jared's prisoners sat in oak chairs, forming a crescent moon in the dining room. Next to them was the dining table, though it had been flipped on its side. The light above them hung on a golden chain, while inside the fixture, two bulbs had been shattered.

The family must have put up a good fight before being tied up.

When my boots stomped inside, Jared swung around without even bothering to raise his gun at me.

"Silver," he said, sounding amused.

I aimed my crossbow at him. "Drop your gun."

He did as he'd been told and let go of his gun. But it didn't fall to the floor. Thanks to its strap, it slid sideways against his thigh and hung there, shimmering under the remaining lightbulbs.

He smiled, and behind him, his men did the opposite—they raised their guns on me, loud clicking sounds filling the house. Behind me, the same sound echoed.

I didn't have to turn around to know my crew had their guns aimed, too.

"I'd say I'm surprised to see you," Jared said, "but I'd be lying."

I glared at him through the sight on my crossbow, aiming for his chest.

"Put your guns down," I said, jerking my

222

chin out at his men. "On the floor."

Jared swung his gun around his back and tightened the strap. He raised two hands next to his dark, scruffy face. "No need for things to get out of hand, here." He tilted his head sideways. "You heard the lady, boys. Put your guns down."

Everyone followed his command and lowered their guns to the floor.

"What are you doing here?" I growled. "Why are you hurting these people?"

With his thumbs tucked inside his belt, he laughed out loud. "Do any of them look hurt to you?"

"You had a gun pointed at that woman's face!" I shouted.

The woman was trembling with tears streaming down her face. Next to her, the man leaned in.

"It's okay, honey, it's okay. We're going to be okay."

She was so distraught it was like she couldn't hear him.

The teenage boy was still glaring at Jared, and I got the feeling that if his restraints were to come undone, he'd lunge straight for his throat. On the floor was a little girl—maybe three years old—with rope around her tiny wrists. It was an awful sight that only made me angrier. What threat did a toddler possibly pose?

On the last chair was a girl who looked a lot like the teenage boy, and it quickly became obvious that these two were siblings—possibly even twins. They both had light golden hair like their mother and lots of freckles on their faces.

Next to her feet were broken plates and pancakes lying across the floor.

It was a sad sight to see. I imagined this family was enjoying a quiet breakfast before Jared stormed in with his men.

"Kick them away," I said, jabbing my loaded crossbow at their guns.

Jared's men grumbled something, but when Jared nodded at them, they kicked their guns across the dark wooden floor.

"You too," I said to Jared.

Smiling, he slipped out of the strap, placed his gun down, and gave it a gentle kick with his boot.

I stared at him for what felt like minutes, wishing I could rip that smile off his face. Part of me wanted to fire the shot. Maybe if we got rid of him and his men, most of our problems would be solved.

But I knew it wasn't right. He wasn't even trying to put up a fight.

That, in itself, was a bit worrisome. I got the feeling he was up to something.

"This whole thing is a misunderstanding,"

Jared said.

Clenching my jaw, I widened my eyes at his gun.

Without breaking eye contact, he kicked it farther this time.

"We'll get out of your hair," he said.

When he started walking toward me, I tightened the grip around my crossbow.

"I'm not going to try anything," he said.

I stepped aside, making way. The sooner he was out of the house, the sooner these people would be safe. Besides, what could they possibly do without their guns? Although Jared often instigated fights, his will to live must have been stronger than his desire to do whatever it was he had come here to do.

I was a bit surprised by how easily he'd backed down, but maybe he'd sensed how badly I wanted to fire that shot—maybe he knew that unlike other people in the bunker, I wouldn't hesitate to kill him.

He let out a sharp whistle and his men followed him. Pipes, however, made his way to the back again. What was he planning on doing? Stealing the dog? Hurting the dog?

"Leave the dog alone," I said.

Jared sneered. "The dog won't get hurt, I promise."

I stepped sideways, my bolt still on Jared as he walked past my group and toward the front door.

"You didn't answer me!" I said. "What were you doing here?"

His men slipped past him, exiting through the front door, while Jared remained inside the house. He smiled and said, "You'll see."

What was that supposed to mean? I wanted to demand answers, but he swung the door open and whistled a tune as he stepped out onto the front porch.

"Please," the woman pleaded, catching my attention.

"Let's untie them," I said.

Everyone hurried into the dining room, crushing bits of broken lightbulbs. James pulled out his knife and began removing the restraints one at a time.

When the man was untied, he rubbed his irritated wrists. Next, the woman was set free, and she threw her arms around the man.

I set my crossbow aside, prepared to untie the young child when a loud, drilling sound filled the house. I couldn't tell where it was coming from. It sounded like it had come from the back, but also, the front.

When I looked at the front door, my stomach sank.

Jared stood in the window, smiling at me and showing me what looked like a drill. He pressed a button, causing that loud zipping sound again. Then, he aimed his drill at the door and started drilling.

What was he doing?

I grabbed my crossbow, prepared to charge at him, when he used his padded elbow to smash the door's small window to bits. Glass shards sprinkled inside the house, and Jared stuck his face in the hole.

"Always wanting to be the hero, Silver." His smile turned into a grimace. "But heroes are a pain in my ass."

He raised what looked like a bottle of wine with fluid inside. An old cloth was tucked in through the neck, soaking up the liquid. He raised a small, silver gadget and pressed a button. At once, a little orange flame appeared and he moved it toward the cloth, lighting it on fire.

I didn't have time to react or even understand what he was doing.

Without warning, he tossed the flaming bottle through the door's broken window and inside the house.

The second it landed, fire splashed in every direction, lighting the floor and the nearest wall on fire.

The flames grew fast, reaching for the ceiling. Through them, I caught a glimpse of Jared still smiling at me through the broken window. It was an evil look that told me this was precisely what he wanted.

At once, he stuck his arm inside and pointed a small gun in our direction. I didn't have time to react. He fired, and Westin cried out in pain before collapsing to the floor. Blood spilled from his thigh, and he covered it with both hands, yet it seeped through his fingers.

I quickly grabbed my crossbow and fired a shot for Jared's face. He pulled away, disappearing from view, but it wouldn't have mattered anyway. My bolt landed hard into the doorframe, nowhere near where Jared's face had been.

If only I'd had a spear to throw.

James ran for the front door with a raised arm, shielding himself from the heat. He grabbed the door handle and shook it hard, but the door didn't open. "Son of a bitch! He trapped us inside!"

When James turned around, menacing flames blew out sideways, climbing the wall next to him.

If we couldn't get out through the front, we had to find another exit.

Pipes, I remembered. *The dog.*

I ran to the back, where Pipes had gone earlier. But right as I turned the corner, I walked into a painful wall of heat. Inside the kitchen, tall flames licked at the cabinets and spread their way up to the ceiling.

There was no getting out this way, either.

I swallowed hard, feeling like I might collapse.

We were sealed inside.

CHAPTER 22

I turned away from the kitchen, the tip of my nose painfully hot.

By the time I rushed back into the dining room area, smoke already filled the air. Westin lay on the floor, groaning in pain as Emma tried to wrap something around his leg.

He threw his head back and breathed heavily through clenched teeth.

I searched the room, hoping to find another exit point. But even the windows were boarded up, and from the looks of it, countless nails had been used to set the wood in place.

A ball of fire suddenly burst out, enveloping the living room sofa. The young child screamed at the sight of it and smashed her red-cheeked face into her mother's leg.

The man scooped up the child in his strong arms. "This way."

Whipping his arm in a circular motion, he rushed his other two children and his wife, urging them to go ahead of him, then guided everyone else down a narrow hallway next to the kitchen.

Soon, this hallway would be up in flames, too.

We had to move fast.

The teenage boy led the way to a white door and opened it. He then stood there, waiting for everyone else to go first.

"Go on, son," the man said.

The boy hesitated, but then ran down the stairs.

James and Adu stood on each side of Westin to help him walk—a challenging task given how large Westin was. With every hop, Westin threw his head back and growled.

We entered a cool, musty stairwell. I followed the boy, cobwebs sticking to my forehead as we descended, but I didn't care. The only thing that mattered was getting away from the fire. The walls that ran along the stairs felt like they were made of stone, though it was hard to see with how dark it was down here. The stairs, however, creaked with every step, which told me they were wooden. Once the fire ate through the door, it would likely descend into the basement. So what was this man's plan? Was there a water supply down here?

"To the cellar!" the man shouted.

Cellar? What cellar?

The teenage boy pushed aside a shelf full of glass jars and buckets, revealing a wooden door that looked centuries old. When he opened it, another dark room appeared, and he stepped inside.

Where had he gone?

Seconds later, natural light flooded the cellar.

A root cellar.

We'd had a similar one in Lutum, only ours was four times the size and used to store food for the people of Division 9. We rushed through it, leaving behind colorful roots and vegetables on wooden shelves. The teenage girl tried to grab a few turnips and squashes, but her father took them out of her arms.

"No," he said, placing them back down on the shelves. "If the cellar survives, we'll come back."

"But—" she tried.

"No, Greta," he said. "We need to travel light."

Greta didn't argue with her father. We exited the cellar rushed toward old wooden stables outside. Behind us, the house was now enveloped in fire, flames reaching out through the cracks in the windows and melting the side panels.

The family looked devasted, but there was

no time to stand there and mourn.

"Farley, get the horses," the man ordered.

"Yes, Papa."

The teenage boy ran toward the stables, and Greta chased after him.

We moved away from the house to steer clear of the flames, when suddenly, explosive blasts filled the air around us. I couldn't tell where it was coming from, but it was loud and inconsistent.

"Get down!" the father shouted.

He grabbed his wife and young daughter, pulling them into the grass, while my people fired back, shooting blindly in every direction.

"Stop it, stop it!" James shouted. "Get down!"

He had to grab Adu by the arm to make him stop firing. The rest listened, lowering their guns and crawling onto their stomachs.

I had no idea what was going on, but James seemed to know.

"It's just ammo," James said. Lying flat on his stomach, he turned to the man. "Do you carry guns and ammo inside?"

The man nodded. "I couldn't get to it in time."

"The fire," James clarified. "It's causing the bullets to explode. It'll stop."

He was right—within seconds, the explosive sounds stopped. As we got back up,

Farley and Greta came galloping toward us on brown and white horses. Farley held on to a lead, guiding another horse with an empty saddle next to him.

The man stood up and approached the horses, petting their large necks.

"I'm Logan Clark," the man said, extending a hand my way.

His hand was firm, which came as no surprise given how sculpted his shoulders were. He was a short man, but he was built like a bull. It was as if he spent every day carrying sheep from one corner of his property to another. His short hair was neither brown nor blond, but somewhere in the middle, while his medium-length beard was gray and unkempt.

"We can do the rest of the introductions later," he said. "Right now, we need to get your friend some medical assistance."

He spoke of medical care as if he had access to it.

Wasn't he alone out here? Did he know a doctor nearby?

"Do you have transportation?" he asked.

"Yes," I said. "But we're about half a mile that way." I pointed away from the burning house, where the rover was hidden.

"We don't have time," Logan said. "We'll take your friend to the village and get him the care he needs. Do you see that path? Follow it until you reach a sign that says, *Lockridge*, then take a right turn into the forest. Don't follow the sign's direction. Turn *right*, not left. The path is wide enough for vehicles. When you get to the front gates, tell them Logan sent you."

He grabbed the extra horse Farley had standing next to him and urged Westin to move closer.

"No need to make any commands," Logan said to Westin. "Let Farley guide the horse."

James and Adu brought him up close, and with Logan's help, they hoisted Westin onto the horse.

He cried out as his leg went over the saddle, then leaned forward, his dark skin looking a few shades paler. Sweat glistened from his forehead and his eyes rolled back. I imagined the pain was excruciating.

"See you soon," Logan said, matter-of-factly.

He handed his little girl to his daughter, Greta, then gave the horse's butt a gentle tap. The two teenagers took off, pulling Westin's horse behind them.

Logan and his wife ran toward the barn and came back out with another two horses. He waved at me in the distance and pointed at the path again. He then whistled, and a large German Shepherd seemingly appeared out of nowhere, following him.

"Did he say *village*?" Sierra asked. She made a face that told me she didn't trust the man. "We should have taken Westin back to our own people."

"We're about an hour away from home," I said. "Their village must be closer."

James sighed. "We can't go back right now. Not after what Jared did. Maybe it's best if he thinks we're dead."

Adu didn't seem to agree. "Jared needs to be held accountable for his actions. I say we go back and tell Elias everything."

"What makes you think he'll believe us?" Emma asked.

Colton, who seemed to always be standing only a few feet away from Emma, crossed his arms over his padded chest. "For all we know, Elias was in on this. I mean, you said it yourself, right, Silver? That Elias is the one who sent you out here."

I thought back to the evening I spent in Elias's room with Finn and Reina. He'd explained everything to me. He'd told me that he planned to have our people unite. Wasn't that the truth? It made sense, after all.

Then, I thought back to Mr. Darwin—my father—and how kind he'd been to me when we first met. Later, he'd threatened me, as well as my grandmother and my mother.

As much as I wanted to believe every word

Elias had told me, Colton was right. We couldn't trust anyone—not after what had happened with Jared. The only people I trusted were Finn and Reina, and they had no authority inside the bunker, which meant they couldn't protect us.

"We're going to the village," I said, marching toward the rover.

No one argued. There was nothing to discuss. Right now, all that mattered was ensuring that Westin was okay. Despite all of the awful people I'd met in my life, I knew there were good people, too. This family—the Clarks—seemed like good people.

We hurried back to the rover and James turned it on.

"Don't go on the path yet," I said.

He reached for his sunglasses on the dashboard and looked at me. "Why not?"

"Jared might still be around," I said. "Waiting for the house to collapse."

"You mean to make sure we're dead," Sierra said coldly.

I glanced back at her but didn't say anything.

Despite her usual calm demeanor, she looked about ready to smash a hole in Jared's face if she ever saw him again. She stared wide-eyed at the back of my seat, her jaw muscles popping.

"Jared will get what he deserves for this," I said. "Right now, let's focus on getting to this village."

James nodded and drove off into the field and around the stables. It wasn't until we'd traveled several miles that he made a sharp turn and got us onto the path. The ride was much smoother on this surface, with fewer unexpected bumps.

We drove for a few minutes until we came up to an old wooden sign that read, *Lockridge*.

It seemed decades old, with vines climbing up its post. The pointed end was aimed away from the dirt path in the forest. But I recalled what Logan had told us: to ignore the sign's direction and to turn right. This was likely a safety precaution to prevent unknown travelers from exploring the path. And, as Logan had assured us, the path looked wide enough for the rover to drive through.

James turned right, moving onto the shaded path. It was clear of any debris and fallen branches, but up ahead, something was blocking the way.

I pointed at the obstacle. "What is that?"

James peered over the top of his sunglasses. "Looks like a gate."

Sure enough, as we moved closer, the metal gate came into view. It was black and rusted, and I expected it to split open as we drove up, but no such thing happened.

Was this a trap, after all?

"State your business," came a muffled voice.

James lowered his window and waited.

"State your business." The voice was much louder this time, but I couldn't tell where it had come from.

"Logan sent us!" James shouted back, his voice echoing throughout the forest.

We waited as his echo faded. Nearby, leaves rustled and birds chirped. Then, a fresh breeze swept through James's open window, filling the entire rover with the smell of earth, cedar, and flowers. Despite the ominous voice shouting at us, this place seemed rather peaceful.

A man and a woman suddenly appeared from out of the forest. They wore blotchy green and brown clothing that made them look invisible next to the trees. I couldn't tell what it was made from. It almost looked like green cotton covered in mud. Around their limbs were thin branches full of green and yellow leaves twirled several times over, and on their skin was more mud. In some areas, it crumbled, revealing a few spots of skin. Where had they been hiding? On the ground?

Without making eye contact, they moved toward the middle of the gate, unlatched something, and pulled. They walked backward as they dragged each gate open, and only then did I notice the spears fastened to their backs.

Unlike ours, theirs weren't made of metal. Instead, the tips appeared to be carved out of bone.

"Who are these people?" Emma asked, leaning forward.

No one responded.

Slowly, we drove past them, our tires splashing mud behind us. The two muddy guards simply stood there with their eyes closed. Or at least, it looked that way. Their faces looked like nothing more than a puddle of mud. No eyes, no lips, no nose that I could see. How had they done that?

"That was weird," Emma said in the back.

Within minutes, we reached the end of the path.

"Holy—" James took off his sunglasses.

I stared straight ahead, my mouth agape.

This was the village?

CHAPTER 23

I couldn't believe what I was seeing.

Houses were painted all sorts of colors—vivid yellow, deep blue, bright pink. Nothing looked dull here. Everything was vibrant and full of life. What surprised me the most were the houses on posts standing above the huge body of water. Why weren't they tipping over?

And what was all this water? A *lake*?

I blinked hard, taking it all in. The water seemed to never end. It was mesmerizing, and I stared at the large body of water, feeling small.

Around the houses were boats of all shapes and sizes. One man with long black braids down his back and a large round belly stepped out of his waddling boat, carrying a large net full of fish.

"Catch of da day!" he shouted.

"Papa, can I see?" said a little girl. She ran up to him, poking at the fish through the net.

Suddenly, the man saw us in the distance and wrapped a protective arm around the little girl. He bent forward and whispered something to her. It made her eyes go big, and she ran as fast as she could inside a purple house.

The man followed her, though he wasn't as fast.

The village itself wasn't very large—easily half the size of Ortus—but it looked self-sufficient.

At once, dozens of people wearing bone crowns and fish skulls around their necks appeared seemingly out of nowhere. Those who had light skin wore black painted stripes across their eyes and nose, while those with dark skin had white stripes. They moved toward us, watching us with intense curiosity. In their grasps were sharp weapons carved from bone—spears, axes, and even clubs with sharp teeth.

They walked in a swaying motion, their heads bowed as if trying to determine our threat level.

"Keep your weapons inside the rover," I ordered.

Sierra didn't seem to like the idea, but she did as I'd instructed.

I stepped out first, raising my hands above my head. "We're here for our friend, Westin. Logan brought him in. We don't want any

244

trouble."

Out from the crowd of mysterious people came a woman with brown skin, short blond hair with shaved sides, white chalk across her eyes, and red markings on her chin. It looked like blood, as if she'd eaten an uncooked animal. She was the only one with this coloring, too.

Maybe it meant something.

She stared at me and elevated her chin, showcasing her strong, prominent jaw. It was an intense look that made me want to climb back into the rover and tell James to turn around.

But I stood my ground.

Logan had sent us here. Surely, this was nothing more than a scare tactic to ensure we weren't the enemy.

"Please," I said. "We only want to know that our friend is okay."

She moved closer to me, jabbing the end of her spear into the sand with every step.

I swallowed hard.

Why was she staring at me like that? It was almost as if she was trying to read my mind. Was she succeeding?

"Name," she said.

It came out sounding like an order.

"S-Silver," I said. "Silverstasia Blackwood."

She elevated her chin even higher. Some of

the white chalk that ran across her eyes also coated some of her eyelashes, giving her an eerie inhuman appearance.

Suddenly, she smiled, her white-painted lips cracking and revealing a bit of pink.

She extended a hand, and when I grabbed it, she shook my entire arm. "Any friend of Logan is a friend of ours."

She held on to my arm for what felt like minutes, still staring at me. "He told us what you did. I cannot thank you enough."

I wasn't sure what Logan meant to this woman, or what kind of relationship they had, but I got the feeling that he played an integral part in this community.

"*Agnu aiko*," the woman said, tilting her head to the side.

I blinked hard.

The man standing next to her ran in the opposite direction, sand splashing up behind his kicking feet.

What had she just said? Had she spoken another language? As terrified as I was to be standing somewhere unknown, away from Sadie and the people I knew, I was excited to hear someone speak a different language.

"Wh-what did you say?" I asked.

She stared at me again. "If I had intended for you to understand, I wouldn't have spoken in my native tongue."

246

Had my question been rude?

"Come," she said, turning around.

We followed her through the quiet village, and one by one, people began to reemerge from their homes. Many watched us with curiosity and fascination, while others seemed too afraid to step out of their houses. Instead, they watched us from behind their glassless windows.

"Welcome to Lockridge," the woman said. "Home of the Loch Ness Monster."

She didn't turn around, so I couldn't tell if she was being serious or trying to be entertaining.

"That's false," Adu whispered. "As the name suggests, the Loch Ness Monster originates from—"

James nudged him in the ribs and he kept quiet.

The nameless woman brought us to a wooden hut at the far back of the village. It had no door, and instead, the entrance was shielded by curtains made of green vegetation.

What was that? Seaweed?

She pointed at me, then swept the vegetation aside. "Only you."

Cautiously, I entered the dark hut. The moment I did, Westin's voice caught me off guard.

"Hey," he moaned.

He lay in a bed against the back wall with a white blanket over his body. Only his head remained visible. His eyes were red and bloodshot, yet he still managed to smile.

He looked genuinely happy to be here. What did he have to be so happy about? He'd been shot in the leg.

"Are you okay?" I asked.

"Oh, yeah," he said, still smiling.

"Sarmina gave him something for the pain," the woman said.

"Who's Sarmina?" I asked.

"The doc," Westin said. "Took good care of me."

He stared at the ceiling, grinning to himself.

"Will he be okay?" I asked.

The woman nodded.

Outside of the hut came more voices, and through the hanging vegetation appeared many different feet.

I walked out to find Logan and his family standing next to James, shaking his hand. It looked like he was thanking us for what we'd done. When Logan spotted me, he hurried over and shook my hand, too.

"I can't thank you enough," he said. "You saved my family."

I wasn't sure how to respond to that. The only reason Jared had tied them up in the first place was to lure me in. But as much as I hated that these people were put in the middle of my feud with Jared, I couldn't blame myself. Jared was the one who had set this whole thing up. He was responsible—not me. And he would pay dearly.

Logan cleared his throat to fill the silence. "This is my wife, Annie," he said, wrapping his arm around her. And this is Greta, my daughter." He pointed at his teenage girl. His pointed finger moved over slightly. "That's my boy, Farley, and this here..." He gently rubbed his little girl's cheek. She smiled sweetly and buried her face in her mother's neck. "This is Haley."

Everyone smiled and nodded at me, thanking me for what I'd done.

"Your friend needs to stay here a few days," Logan said. "Sarmina gave him some potent herbs to treat any potential infection."

"How do you know these people?" I asked.

Logan smirked at the nameless woman.

"Ari and I met over ten years ago," he said.

I turned to the woman—Ari—who looked sweetly at him. It was an expression I knew she'd never give me.

"I owe her everything," he said.

He went quiet as if reliving whatever had happened between them. He then wrapped his arm around his wife, kissed her ash-stained forehead, and said, "Several years ago, my wife got sick. I searched the wastelands for a doctor. I became dehydrated and sickly myself and collapsed near the forest."

"My people found him and brought him to us," Ari said. "And since then, he's never stopped showing us gratitude." She paused, smiled at the Clark family, and even squeezed Greta's shoulder. It was obvious they'd grown close over the years. "Every few months, Logan brings us fruits and vegetables from his garden, even though his debt has already been paid in full."

"This isn't to pay any debt," Logan said. "I'm thankful."

I wanted to ask Logan if he'd be staying here with his family from now on, but I didn't have the time. In seconds, a strange sound caught everyone's attention, and they turned their heads sideways.

Out from the same path we'd entered from came a long, yellow vehicle with dozens of windows, a black hood, and big black tires. Over the front window were a few letters far away from each other: S and L. It was apparent that the letters in between had fallen off.

"Get inside," Ari warned.

Logan wrapped his arms around his family and urged them to enter the medical hut. I stared at the rover, wishing we hadn't left our weapons behind. I wasn't certain we'd need them, but judging based on Ari's tone, I had the impression this guest wasn't a friend.

"Who is that?" I asked.

"Get inside," Ari warned through clenched teeth.

I did as I'd been told and urged the others to follow me. We huddled inside, breathing in hot, humid air, and waited. I stepped close to the seaweed curtain and rested my face against it, peering through.

The strange vehicle didn't even bother coming out of the forest. It parked next to our rover, with its butt still hidden within the trees. How long was that thing?

"Ari!" came a loud, obnoxious voice.

Out from the vehicle stepped a short man with big round glasses, curly brown hair, a protruding belly, and a bright blue jacket that matched some of Lockridge's colorful houses. He walked with a strut as if he and Ari were best friends.

As she approached him with her spear, however, the short man stuck out a flat palm and jabbed a stubby finger toward the ground. It was a gesture meant to say, *Put your weapon down.*

They were definitely *not* friends.

Bending her knees, Ari lowered her spear into the sand.

Her other people—the ones with face paint

and bone weapons—did the same thing.

Once everyone's weapons were lowered, the man's pasty lips stretched into a grin. He stood on his tippytoes and swayed back and forth like he was having the time of his life. "What do you have for me today? Tuna, I hope!"

Ari whistled, and from near the dock came a teenage boy carrying a wooden crate. Although I couldn't see inside, silver scales shimmered on the surface.

What was that? A crate full of fish?

"Everything okay, boss?" came a strangely distant voice.

"Yes, yes," the man shouted, waving a hand at his large vehicle. "It's okay, soldiers. Everything is fine! Stay inside."

Who was he talking to? The yellow vehicle's windows were mucky, like it had been driven through deep puddles of mud. I leaned in, trying to get a better look. Then, I saw something. Through the filthy windows were the silhouettes of people—heads. It was all I could see. Oddly, the heads all appeared to be the same size. Were those helmets? Were those really soldiers in there? If so, how many soldiers were there?

The young boy approached Ari and placed the crate in the sand by her feet.

"Bring it here," the chubby man said.

The boy hesitated, but Ari gave him a nod,

reassuring him. So the boy brought the crate right up to the stranger. With short, swollen fingers, the man reached inside and pulled out a dead fish. He waved it around in the air a few times, then raised it above his puffy, curly locks, and inspected it. "This is cod."

He didn't sound impressed.

As he inspected it, something gold sparkled on his fingers. Rings?

"And it looks to be a few days old," he said.

"You're a day early," Ari pointed out.

The man's smile vanished, and an ugly sour look replaced it. "We're midafternoon," he growled. "Don't you people fish in the morning?"

Ari stiffened her stand and locked her fingers in front of her belly. Although I could only see her dark, muscular back from here, I imagined she was giving him the same unimpressed look she'd given me earlier. As the sun shone down on her head, her short blond hair looked white.

"This is our offering," she said coldly.

The short man glowered at her, looking like he was contemplating dumping the entire crate of fish on her head.

With a huff, he turned around. "I expect tuna next week."

Ari didn't respond, which seemed to anger the man.

"Are we clear?" he snarled, snapping his head sideways.

She gave him a firm nod.

The man climbed back into his yellow machine and a loud rumble filled the air. Slowly, the vehicle moved backward, disappearing into the trees.

CHAPTER 24

A ri came back toward the medical hut with flared nostrils and a clenched jaw. "Krampus is still alive?" Logan asked.

She nodded. "Unfortunately."

"Krampus?" I asked.

Ari rolled her eyes. "As much as I despise the man, he's the only thing keeping that wall"—she pointed her nose at the lake—"from obliterating our village."

"Wall? What wall?" I blurted.

Did she know about *that* wall, too? She couldn't possibly be talking about the invisible wall, could she? How many people knew about that thing?

Logan bowed his head. "Earth's end."

"Earth's end?" I said.

Sierra stepped toward Logan. "So you know about the wall, too? What do you know of it?"

Both Logan and Ari looked confused. Annie, Logan's wife, took this as an opportunity to escape the conversation. She'd probably heard the discussion several times. Scooping up her young toddler, she left toward the dock, and Farley and Greta followed her.

"We know it was made by people," Ari said. "We also know someone is controlling it."

"What do you mean, *controlling* it?" I asked. "And what does Krampus have to do with the wall?"

"Come," Ari said.

She led the group to the lake's shore. Every time the foamy white water washed up over the sand, pink, white, and beige shells appeared. It took everything in me not to run up to them and pick them up. I'd always wondered what shells felt like against the fingers.

In the sky, birds flew circularly over the water, crying loudly before diving in headfirst.

I smiled at the sight, then reached for a pink shell next to my toe. It was cool, incredibly soft, and shimmered a shade of green when I twirled it.

"Pretty, isn't it?" James asked.

He had his sunglasses back on.

"Why do you always wear those?" I asked.

He shrugged. "Makes me feel safe. You wouldn't know it looking at me, but I have pretty bad social anxiety."

I was about to ask him what that was when

Ari raised her hand over her brows, shielding the afternoon sun from her face. She stared at the horizon, where if you looked closely enough, you could see little ripples in the air, distorting the sky.

"You see that?" she said.

Everyone stared. It was subtle, but we'd seen it before. It was a strange effect that made me question reality. What lay beyond that wall? Was there even anything? I could see through it, but there was no getting past it. Was the other side nothing more than an illusion?

"The world ends at that wall," she said.

I blinked hard. "How do you know?"

Lowering her hand, she looked back at me as if I were foolish to question such a thing. "Because there's no going past it. Therefore, there's nothing beyond the wall."

How could she even say something like that? In Lutum, we were confined by concrete walls. Outside of the walls, however, were many areas to explore, including Lockridge—a village I would have never known about if I hadn't left Lutum.

"How do we know that?" I said. "Maybe there is and we just can't get to it."

She cocked a brow and glanced sideways at Logan, likely regretting having allowed me inside the village. She probably wasn't accustomed to having someone ask so many questions.

But what was the point of anything if we didn't ask questions? It was how we learned, or at least, how I learned. Without questions, people couldn't grow.

"It simply is," Ari said.

I wasn't satisfied with that answer, but I bit my tongue.

"Krampus has contact with the creator," she continued. "In exchange for goods, he ensures that the wall doesn't move toward us. If it did, it would mean the end of all of us."

I had so many questions running through my mind.

For one, how did Ari know she could trust this Krampus man? What if he was lying? Did she have proof that what he said was true? I must have been making a puzzled face; Ari gave me a smug look and said, "You have doubts."

I had more than doubts.

I didn't believe a word of it.

If this Krampus man could move the wall, why not move it away, and expand our lands? It didn't make any sense. And threatening to destroy a village didn't make sense, either. Not if he was benefiting from the village.

"How long has he been collecting resources from you?" I asked.

Ari sighed. "As long as I can remember."

"As long as I've known you," Logan said.

"At least a decade," Ari added.

"Has he ever hurt anyone?" I asked.

Ari scowled at me. It was as if she was getting tired of being interrogated.

"The man has an entire bus full of armed soldiers prepared to slaughter our people," she said coldly. "I've never gave him the opportunity to hurt anyone."

"Have you ever seen them?" I asked. "The soldiers, I mean."

I wasn't even sure why I was so inquisitive. It must have been because something had felt off about the whole meeting—the way Krampus spoke, the clothes he wore, and even his *bus* full of soldiers.

"What's your point, child?" she asked.

I didn't appreciate being called a child, but I knew she was only frustrated. For years, the people of Lockridge had been living a certain way, submitting to Krampus's demands. And now, a stranger questioned them about it. No doubt, it made her defensive.

"You're prisoners," I said.

She moved toward me, fists clenched. "We are not prisoners."

"Well, kind of," I said. "You have someone who takes from you and doesn't give back."

"He assures us protection," she said.

"But what if it isn't true?" I asked.

Ari's jaw dropped as if I just told her fish

could walk on land. She seemed insulted by my suggestion.

Her dark eyes narrowed on me. "What if *what* isn't true?"

"That this Krampus man has any power over the wall," I said. "I mean, my best guess is that the wall was designed by the Elites, and that guy definitely didn't look like an Elite—"

"The Elites," Ari breathed. "How do you know of this legend?"

I arched a brow and looked at my fellow fighters. *Legend*? I'd never heard anyone refer to the Elites as a legend.

James cleared his throat. "Silver comes from that area."

Ari's eyes went huge. "Have you seen one?"

Was she referring to an Elite? I'd seen plenty. They looked like everyone else. I wondered what kind of folklore traveled through the lands. Clearly, Ari and her people didn't travel. Or, maybe they had at some point and had seen the city of Olympus, but had known better than to venture too close.

"Will you feast with us?" Ari asked. "I'd love to hear about it."

Although I didn't want to talk about Lutum or Olympus, I smiled courteously and agreed. Logan called out to his wife, and Ari waved a hand at someone. I couldn't tell what she was doing until a horn sounded across the village, and one by one, people began to reemerge from their homes.

"Let me introduce you to my people," she said, smiling back at us.

CHAPTER 25

The large fire danced in a pit, surrounded by sand.

I leaned forward, allowing the heat to warm my cheeks, my nose, my neck. People moved about freely, socializing with my fighters, Logan, and his family. They had so many questions.

After having shared with everyone my story of Lutum, I felt exhausted and no longer wanted to talk. So I sat in silence, watching the stars overhead and wondering if Sadie was thinking of me, too.

Across from me, Ari watched me with fascination. Every time I caught her staring, the corner of her mouth tugged up and she took a sip from her custom Lockridge beverage—something I had politely declined.

The red and white markings on her face were gone; she'd washed them off in the lake before supper. When I had asked her about it, she explained that one could never be too prepared to face off against threats, and that looking intimidating was an advantage they chose to utilize.

Now that nightfall had approached, she and her people felt they didn't need the markings.

Ari was a unique-looking woman with a slim figure yet defined muscles. She carried herself upright, with a confident posture that I knew her people would follow anywhere.

"Are you all right?" she finally asked me over the sound of children giggling.

One young boy fell against her leg, and she laughed out loud—a reaction I hadn't expected.

The mother was quick to apologize and scoop up her son.

"I'm okay," I said, even though this wasn't true. I'd lost myself in my thoughts again—thoughts of Grandma, of Mother, and Lutum. I thought of Olympus, and how people spoke of it as if royalty lived there. I wanted to scream to the entire world—tell them that they were all wrong. The Elites were no different from anyone else, aside from the serum running through their veins.

"I'm sorry," she said softly.

My eyes shot up at her. What was she apologizing for? She'd saved my new friend, Westin, and had kindly given Logan and his family shelter.

She must have sensed my confusion; she smiled sweetly and added, "For the life you've lived."

"At least I'm alive," I said.

She seemed to admire these words. She took another sip of her beverage and placed the bone cup into the sand by her feet.

"Tonight, you are not Silver of Lutum," she said. "Nor are you a Breeder from Olympus." She got up, walked around the fire, and stuck out a hand. "Tonight, you are Silverstasia of Lockridge."

Her eyes sparkled, reflecting the fire's orange flame.

When I grabbed her arm, she pulled me up, and at once, drums thumped nearby. Everyone joined in, clapping and chanting, and I stood awkwardly as a few Lockridge citizens stomped their feet in the sand and danced to the rhythm of the beat.

Ari clapped her hands, then reached for my wrists and made me clap mine.

It made me feel like a child again, but I liked it. For the first time in a long time, I didn't think about the dangers around me, or about how we were going to survive tomorrow. All that mattered was the music and the happy expressions bouncing all around me.

Eventually, I started clapping on my own and stomping my bare feet in the sand.

Even James joined in. He pulled his pant legs up his shins and stomped with such strange movements, I couldn't help but laugh. He kicked grains of sand all over the place, but he didn't seem to care.

Ari shouted something and laughed, encouraging everyone to follow James's new dance.

We celebrated for what felt like hours as the moon ascended high into the sky, casting a white glow across the water.

I woke up to the sound of seagulls squawking in the distance. Next to me, James sat up, rubbing his crusted eyes.

"Hey," he moaned, looking sideways at me.

I slowly got up, remembering that I was no longer in Fort Denton, but rather, in Lockridge.

The air around me felt warm and moist. A gentle breeze swept through the partially closed curtain of our hut, filling the space with the smell of earth and fish. It wasn't yet bright out, but the gray-orange light coming through the cracks of our shelter told me the sun was only now beginning to rise.

Nearby, voices filled the air.

They were soft, at first, but then people began to move toward the water and walked along creaking docks.

"Get the boats ready," one man said.

"Do you have the nets?" a woman asked.

The man laughed at her but didn't respond.

One by one, more of our fighters began to wake up. The shelter we'd been given was temporary—a hut typically used for storing food and goods—but it had been enough to protect us from the environment. Ari had pushed all of their supplies to one side of the hut, giving us ample space to sleep on the opposite end. The bed underneath me was nothing more than a large blanket stuffed with cotton, and although it was unsightly, it had provided me a good night's rest.

"We should head back," I said.

James nodded, as did everyone else. Westin hadn't spent the night with us. As Ari had told us, and as Dr. Sarmina had later confirmed, Westin would need to stay here for at least a week while he recovered.

As we emerged from the hut, Logan approached us with his wife. Behind him, Ari followed, her face once more painted with red and white markings.

One by one, Logan shook our hands.

"Thank you," he repeated to each of us. "We owe you everything."

"Thank you," I returned. "You saved our friend's life."

While everyone started chatting about what happened, Ari approached me.

"Will you be returning to pick him up? Or would you like us to send him with an escort?" she asked.

I smiled at her generosity. "We're quite a ways from here. With the rover, we can travel quickly. We'll come back."

I turned away from the others and Ari followed, her shoulders hunched forward as if to block our voices from everyone else.

"If we don't return—" I said.

Her thin brows met above the bridge of her nose.

I sighed. "I don't know what's going to happen in Fort Denton. The man who went after Logan's family happens to be the brother of the man in charge."

She seemed surprised by this, likely wondering why I would ever return to such a treacherous place.

"Elias is a good man," I said quickly, but then I hesitated. "At least, I hope he is. But there's no telling what will happen when we return. Jared may have told everyone we died. He may not have. I don't know what his plan is."

"Will you report what he's done?" she asked.

"Of course." I wasn't sure what other option she thought I had. Jared had done something terrible, and the people of Fort Denton deserved to know. I didn't plan on hiding that from anyone.

The real question was whether or not anyone would believe me.

If Jared got away with this, we were all in grave danger.

Ari rested a dark hand with white painted dots on my shoulder. "You will return, Silver of Lutum."

It was the first time anyone had announced my birthplace with such pride. Any other time Lutum was spoken of, the topic of slavery soon followed. But the way she said it made me feel as though I shouldn't be ashamed of where I'd come from, but rather, empowered by it.

I smiled sweetly at her and thanked her for her taking us in.

She whistled and pointed at a middle-aged man inside her village. He came running, his lanky legs scissoring as sand blasted up around his ankles. "Yes, Ari?"

"Bring these fine people some food for their travels," she said.

"Oh, no, that's okay—" I tried.

Ari gave me her death stare and I shut my mouth. When she turned back to face the man who had come running, I noticed a sly smirk pulling on one side of her mouth. Maybe she enjoyed intimidating others.

"Crab cakes, fruit. Fill up a crate," she ordered.

The man nodded and took off.

"That's very generous of you," James said.

Ari beamed, revealing teeth as white as the markings on her face. "You saved a man who has provided my people food for years, which in turn, has saved us. Therefore, food is the least I can offer." She paused, watching me. "But I do have one request."

I waited.

"Keep our village a secret from your people."

"Why?" I asked.

"This world is a dangerous place, Silver. One of your own tried to kill you. If your people learn about our village, they may send recruits to scavenge our resources."

She wasn't wrong, especially after what had happened with Jared. It was safer to keep this place a secret.

I promised her our secrecy and thanked her again as we loaded the crate into the rover.

Ari and Logan led us to the village's entry point, prepared to send us off. Before climbing into the rover, however, I turned to Ari.

"What about Krampus?" I asked. "We never finished discussing—"

"You let me worry about Krampus," she said. "It would appear you have much bigger problems."

I wanted to help, but she was right. I had to get back to Fort Denton and expose Jared for what he was.

"See you in a week?" I asked.

She nodded. "See you in a week, Silver."

With that, I climbed into the rover and the others did the same. Behind me, Emma and Adu fought over the crate of food sitting on Sierra's lap.

Sierra stared straight ahead with flat eyelids, looking like an annoyed mother surrounded by toddlers.

Ari and Logan waved at us as we turned around and made our way back onto the dirt path in the forest. We didn't have to stop in front of the gate this time. It was immediately opened for us, and we sped through.

"We're low," James said the moment we exited the forest.

"Low?" I repeated.

He pointed his nose at the charge gauge in front of him. I leaned over, noticing the measurement; the measurement bars had turned yellow, slightly below the halfway point.

"Will we make it back?" I asked.

James bit his lip. "I hope so."

CHAPTER 26

Crumbs bounced off the fighters' laps as they ate everything in the crate.

"This is good stuff," Adu mumbled, his mouth half-full of fresh berries.

"How's the gauge?" I asked.

James shook his head as a way of saying, *Not good.*

"Why don't you drive faster, then?" I asked.

He shook his head again. "I'm trying to preserve energy. Going fast burns more energy."

It made the trip feel even longer than our initial journey. Hours passed as we traversed the open field near the river.

"It's not looking good," James said.

I leaned over again. Now, the gauge colors were orange—almost red.

"We need to get over the river," I said.

"I know," James grumbled.

He tightened his grip around the steering

wheel and his freckled knuckles turned white.

What if we didn't make it? How were we supposed to get across the river? The current was strong. Could we swim through it?

"Um, guys," Emma said. "Is that the ramp?"

Everyone leaned forward, squinting.

"It looks funny," Adu pointed out.

James took off his glasses and slowed down as we approached the ramp.

The sight made me sick to my stomach.

"It's... busted," James said.

I blinked hard, thinking my heart might stop. "Busted? What does that even mean?"

"Broken, destroyed, caput," James said.

"How is that even—" I started, but then it hit me.

Jared.

Not only had he tried to kill us and innocent people, but he'd also destroyed our way back. Had he done this in case we survived? Or was this his way of ensuring no one ever went over the river again?

James pulled up next to the broken ramp and everyone got out. Some areas were completely demolished, while others appeared black and charred. The metal beams Westin had carried even appeared to be melted at some ends.

"What happened?" I said.

"Probably a grenade," Sierra said. "They

274

could have dropped it as they were going over."

"Why the hell would they do that?" Colton said. "This side of the river has wheat!"

Everyone started pacing and bickering.

"Let's just rebuild it," Emma said.

Adu scoffed at her. "Rebuild it? There's nothing to rebuild. We don't have replacement materials."

I peered over the other side of the river, where the other ramp stood tall. It hadn't been damaged, which proved to me that Jared didn't care about people going over the river; he didn't want us coming back in the event we survived.

"Why would he do this?" I asked, more to myself than anyone else.

We paced for a while longer, trying to come up with ways to cross the river.

"The rover will have to stay here," James said.

"And what about Westin?" Emma asked. She tucked a strand of blond hair behind her ear. "We're supposed to come back in a week."

James raised two flat palms. "One thing at a time. First, we need to get back to the bunker and deal with Jared. Then, we can come up with a way to cross over again."

"James is right," I said. "Can everyone here swim?"

Everyone nodded.

"Good," I said. "That's a start." Then, I paused, feeling stupid.

Everyone here could swim—everyone but *me*.

"I'll help you over," Sierra said, throwing her chin out at me. "I saw you in the pool."

I felt embarrassed.

"Thanks," I mumbled.

We descended a slope toward the river, weeds and cattails rubbing against our legs. As I watched the foamy white surface of the water, I wasn't so sure I wanted to cross it.

"Current will pull you," Sierra said, "no matter how strong you are."

What did she mean by *pull*? Would I get sucked underwater? Would it become impossible to resurface? Suddenly, I found myself rethinking the idea of swimming across the river. Surely, we could come up with another plan.

"I'll do my best to get us across, but you'll need to kick, too," she said.

"Kick?" I repeated.

"You're freaking her out," James said. He pointed at the river. "See where the water is going? To the right? If you were to jump in there right now, you'll flow along with that current. The goal is to swim across without flowing too far down the river or without getting stuck in the middle."

"Stuck?" I repeated. "How could I get stuck?"

"If the current is too strong," James said. "We won't know for sure until we're in there."

"This is a foolish idea," Adu said.

Everyone looked at him. He ran a hand through his short black locks, then grabbed his forehead and squeezed as if trying to get his brain to work harder. "There are too many uncertain variables. We have no way of knowing the current's velocity, nor—"

"Would you speak in English?" Sierra said, looking at him stupidly.

Adu pointed at the river. "Uncertain current strength. We could easily be swept away by the current."

"What if we use a rope?" James said. "We could connect ourselves—"

"Foolish," Adu said. "I understand your logic, but if we have a few weak links"—he glanced at me and I felt singled out—"then we risk the lives of everyone else."

James threw his arms in the air. "What choice do we have, Adu? We need to get across!"

Adu rubbed at his hairless chin for a moment, no doubt trying to come up with another solution.

He pondered for what felt like an eternity.

I searched the area around us, hoping to

find something that might steer us in the right direction. But there was nothing. The bridge's broken pieces—as well as what remained of the ramp—were useless to us. Nothing was long enough to use as a bridge.

As far as I could tell, even a tree trunk wouldn't be long enough.

Sighing, I said, "We need to get across, and the only way is to swim."

No one argued.

"I'll go first," James said.

But rather than move toward the river, he turned around and returned to the rover. From the back, he extracted what looked like a bunched-up rope.

"What's that for?" Adu asked.

"If all goes well on my end," James said, "I'll be prepared to help one of you out if the current is too strong."

His eyes lingered on me.

"What if *you* get caught in the current?" Sierra asked.

James shrugged like that wasn't even an option.

"I won't." He slipped off his boots and began removing the protective pads from his uniform—off his knees, his elbows, his shins. He even slipped out of his chest plate.

"You should do the same," he said. "The lighter you are, the easier it will be to swim."

Everyone did as James suggested, stripping useless weight from their bodies.

James even went as far as to lay his gun in the grass.

"When I give you the okay," James said, looking at Sierra, "start throwing the guns over."

She nodded briskly.

I stared across the river, wondering how hard she'd have to throw to get each gun across. The width of the river looked about ten or fifteen yards—wide enough to make this task difficult, but not too wide as to prevent us from throwing things over.

Carefully, James slid down the riverbank, dragging his fingertips through the long grass behind him. Crispy vegetation broke as he slid, and when he reached the bottom, he turned to look at us. He removed his sunglasses and tucked them into his pocket. "See you on the other side."

With that, he plunged into the river and started flailing his arms as fast as he could. But it seemed that no matter how hard he swam, the current was stronger. It pulled him sideways as he moved forward.

"It's okay," Sierra said, likely sensing my anxiety. "He's still moving forward, and that's what matters."

Water splashed in every direction, white

froth masking James's location. It wasn't until he reached the other side—quite a ways down to the right—and gripped onto the ledge that I finally breathed out.

Emma cheered as James climbed up the slope and pumped both fists in the air.

"It's not too bad!" he shouted from across. "Use your legs and don't stop swimming!"

Having witnessed James succeed, the others seemed more confident. First, Sierra began tossing the guns over. They landed all over the place on the other side, and James walked from side to side, collecting them.

Adu was next.

He did as James had done and swam hard, creating froth and foam all around his thrashing limbs.

Like James, he successfully reached the other side. James helped him up out of the water, and waved over at us, encouraging the rest of the group to follow.

By the time it was my turn, I looked at Sierra, hoping she might change her mind and agree to attempt to build a new ramp. But I knew this was an irrational thought. It wasn't even an option. We didn't have the materials, and now that everyone was over the river, we certainly didn't have enough hands.

"You can do this," she said. "Just hold on to my belt"—she grabbed her belt and tugged to show me how firm it was—"and keep kicking."

In theory, it sounded simple enough. But I'd nearly drowned in a pool without any current whatsoever. What made her think I'd succeed in reaching the other side without going under the water?

"Use your arms, too," she said. "Rotate them and push the water. And with your legs, try to kick water away from you."

I nodded, even though I was only half listening. The rest of my focus was glued to the river's deep blue—almost green—color, its powerful current, and the sound of water splashing and burbling as it swept along.

"You ready?" she asked.

I wasn't, but I didn't have a choice. We had to get back to the bunker and warn the others about Jared.

"Hold on tight," she said.

At the other end of the river, James stood with what appeared to be a log in his grasp. He showed it to me, and a rope dangled from it, reaching the ground.

"If anything happens," he shouted. "Grab this!"

Was he referring to the log? Would he use it to pull us to safety?

Swallowing hard, I followed Sierra down the riverbend.

"Why did you offer to bring me on the other

side?" I asked.

Sierra looked strong, with a solid back and sturdy shoulders. Colton, however, was even larger than Sierra and probably quite a bit stronger. So why hadn't he been the one to bring me over?

"I'm a strong swimmer," she said confidently. Then, she smirked sideways at me—something I rarely saw her do. "Even better than James, although he'll never admit it."

I didn't say anything, but I believed her.

"Don't let go," she warned me.

Together, we stepped into the river. It was painfully cold and made me breath in sharply through clenched teeth.

Ignore the pain, I told myself. *Get to the other side.*

"Ready?" she said.

I didn't answer.

She plunged forward and I followed, my feet no longer touching river stones. But I did as she'd instructed—I held on tight to her belt and kicked my legs as hard as I could.

"Try to *push* the water with scissoring motions," she said, water hiding her chin. "Don't just kick through it."

I knew she'd said that because I was making things harder on her. So I changed my approach as we moved closer to the strong current and started scissoring with my legs.

"All right, here we go!" she said.

When we swam into the strong current, everything changed. I felt myself being dragged away from her. It was awful and I felt powerless. Water slipped into my mouth, coating my tongue and wetting my dry throat.

I held on tight, but it felt like we were being torn in opposite directions. The water suddenly twirled me over and my arm twisted. With my other hand, I reached for her belt and grabbed on. She swam hard—sometimes quickly without warning—making me almost lose my grip.

"Keep kicking!" she shouted.

As she swam, James and the others appeared to shift to the left.

What was going on? Were we moving down with the current? I had expected this to happen, but it felt like we were going much farther than the others had gone.

"Don't look at them!" Sierra shouted.

Water splashed between us, making it nearly impossible to see her. "Focus straight ahead."

I kicked and slapped my arms through the water, fighting to stay afloat more than anything.

But suddenly, Sierra thrusted hard again, and at the same time, the current spun me onto my back, twisting my arm once again. I tried to switch hands, but it was no use. Just as I reached to grab her, my fingers let go and I began to float away from her, down with the current.

CHAPTER 27

In the distance, people shouted, but I couldn't make out what they were saying.

Around me, the sound of water splashed, bubbled, and fizzed, filling my ears and disorienting me. Every few seconds, the water pulled me under, and all sound faded. It was only when I resurfaced that I could hear my friends calling out to me, their voices sounding like a crowd behind a closed door.

I gasped loudly, filling my lungs with air.

Was I drowning?

Everything happened so fast that I didn't know what to do. I wasn't even sure how far I'd gone, or when it would stop. Would it ever stop? How far did this river go, and where did it end? Was there even an end?

With wide eyes, I searched the sky and the nearby trees, hoping I might find a way out.

But there was no way out. The current was too strong. No matter how hard I fought to reach the other side, it was as if the water had a mind of its own—as if it intended to keep me its prisoner. To make matters worse, it felt like every time I tried to escape, the river punished me by pulling me underwater. It became easier to float on my back and hope that this nightmare would end.

"Silver!"

The voice had sounded a bit closer this time.

I searched the riverbank, then shifted my gaze up the slope to find James running in long strides, holding the log and rope above his head. He ran so fast it was a wonder he didn't smash into a tree. Yet, somehow, he jumped from side to side as he navigated the band of trees on the other side.

He managed to get ahead of me. Leaning back to gain force, he threw the log straight ahead. Behind it, the rope followed, wavering through the air.

The small log landed in the water, bobbing around with the current. It hadn't landed in the middle, though—it sat a bit to the side.

"Grab it!" he shouted.

Panic flashed in James's eyes as he kept feeding rope into the river, trying to center the log. At first, I thought maybe he feared I'd never reach the log, but I quickly realized why he was panicking—a forest stood tall on his side of the river, which meant that soon, he wouldn't be able to follow me.

"Grab it!" he shouted, his voice strained.

Suddenly, James tightened his grip and the log stopped moving. It sat in the water, fighting the current while jiggling from side to side. Foam collected around it, masking it from sight.

Where had it gone?

I slapped the surface of the water, trying to feel for something hard.

"Grab it!" he shouted again.

Then, I spotted it. But I couldn't reach it. I kicked and swam as hard as I could, blinding myself with splashes of water.

I started slapping all around me again until my fingers hit something hard.

The log!

But my fingers had only grazed it. By the time I tried to swing for it again, it was floating behind me. I looked up at James, wanting to apologize for having failed. We locked eyes as he stood there, holding on to the rope and looking devastated.

But his features quickly hardened, and he did something that took me by surprise.

He jumped onto the large, jagged stones on the side of the river and hopped three of them at once. It was a dangerous move—one that could have easily led him into the same position as me.

He wasn't giving up.

Those three steps alone got the log moving toward me again.

Now, I had to play my part.

I did what felt impossible and started swimming *against* the current, hoping to be reunited with the log. It didn't stop me from moving with the water, but it slowed me down enough for the log to catch up with me.

Right when James's rope ran out of slack, I swung my arm as far as I could, my fingers gripping the log.

I squeezed it as tightly as I could against my chest, blinking hard. My heart pounded against the wood, and everything around me spun. Would I make it? Would I come out of this alive?

The current now fought against both me and the log, and James struggled up on his rock. He leaned backward, his arms shaking and his face darkening to a deep red.

Even if I managed to hold on, I wasn't so sure he'd make it.

How could he? He was fighting against the current from an awkward angle. Had he been beside me, then maybe he could have pulled me to shore. But where he stood, all he could do was hold on to me to keep me from floating farther down the river.

Part of me wanted to let go of the log. If I didn't, I was afraid he might slip and join me in the river. That wasn't right, and he certainly didn't deserve to die for trying to save me.

Maybe I'd find a way out farther down the river. I had to try. I had to do something, because I knew James wouldn't let go, not until he fell in with me.

I let go with one hand, and James cried out to me.

"No, Silver, hold on!"

Right before I let go with the other, Sierra and the rest of the gang came running behind him, hopping up onto the rocks. Colton grabbed the rope in front of James and his face swelled as he pulled back as hard as he could.

Sierra and Emma grabbed the slack near James's foot and hurried behind him, fastening it to a tree.

Once the rope was secure, Adu also joined in, pulling until he almost fell into the forest.

"Swim to the side!" James shouted, still shaking.

Rather than try to join them at the rocks, I swam sideways.

They tugged hard on the rope, and somehow, it worked. The resistance was enough to get me out of the strong current and into the river's more gentle current. From there, I managed to kick until I reached the rocky side.

Underneath me was a wall of slimy rocks and seaweed, making it difficult to catch my footing. It was also too steep to climb, so instead, I swam toward the gang as they pulled me on the log.

When I reached it, James bent down, grabbed my hand, and pulled me out of the water. As soon as I was up onto the boulder with him, he pulled me in for a hug. It was a warm embrace, despite our cold, wet clothes.

"Almost lost you," he said.

I forced a smile. "You saved me."

He gave me a sly look and shrugged—a gesture that told me he didn't think it was a big deal. "Team effort."

I didn't understand why he was downplaying it. Friends or not, he'd risked his life to save mine. "You could have died trying to help me."

"Wouldn't you have done the same thing if I was the one drowning?" he asked.

I gave him back the log. "Well, I wouldn't have thought to tie a log—"

"That's not the point," he said. "Would you have tried everything you could?"

I nodded. "Of course."

"Why? Because we're friends?" He raised a brow. "What if I were a total stranger? Would you have let me drown?"

"Of course not. I would have tried everything just the same."

"Why?" he asked.

I paused, thinking it over. "Because it's the right thing to do."

He patted me on the shoulder and said, "Bingo."

CHAPTER 28

Although no door opened for us as we approached, I knew we were almost at the bunker. I recognized the entrance area thanks to a crab apple tree with missing bark.

Farther back were numerous trees, where a forest began—the same forest that traveled all the way to the river. I imagined the courtyard was hiding somewhere in there, with its protective concrete walls.

"Will they even let us in through this door?" I asked as we approached the crab apple tree.

James rolled his shoulder, repositioning his gun on his back. "They will unless Jared told them not to. We don't know what story he spun."

"Is there another door we can use?" I asked.

James looked at me through his dark shades. "We have a few, but they're mostly used as exit points. Elias prefers anyone entering the bunker does so at the main entrance or in the parking lot. It keeps everyone safe. The only problem is, we don't have the rover, so I don't have any way to open that door."

"Don't they monitor?" I asked. "I'm sure someone will see us."

"Not strictly," Sierra said. She scratched at the dark, shaved side of her head. The other side was frizzy and still drying. "We're safe underground. It's not like we need guards monitoring the bunker twenty-four hours a day."

I thought back to the day of the tornado and how Elias had saved us from the storm.

Had it been a fluke? Had they been monitoring the storm, only to see our colony approach? Had it not been for the storm, maybe we wouldn't be alive.

We moved closer to the tree, stepping over rotting crab apples in the grass.

"Can't we knock somewhere?" I asked.

"Give it a minute," James said. "If someone is watching, they'll open the door—"

Suddenly, the massive door creaked open, splitting the earth apart. It was the same door through which we'd entered with the people of Ortus. For some reason, I expected Elias would be the one to greet us.

As the door opened, a man's black boots

came into view. Next, his black pants, his black shirt, and his pale white skin. He leaned against the wall behind him. It was a nonchalant stance that made me recognize the man before even seeing his face.

Jared.

Then, his ugly features came into view.

He stood with his bony arms crossed over his chest and a sly look on his face. Since I'd last seen him, he'd allowed some dark facial hair to grow out. It made him look even meaner, though a bit less sickly.

Down from within the large concrete tunnel came some of his men. They marched, holding their guns to their chests, their jaw muscles popping out, likely hoping Jared might give them the order to blow my head off.

"You're missing one," Jared said, pointing his nose at us. "What happened? Did he get caught in a fire?"

He smiled suggestively.

"You piece of—" I started, rushing toward him.

Colton and Sierra stopped me, but Jared didn't even flinch.

Instead, he looked at his dirty fingernails, then rubbed them against his padded chest. "I have to say, Silver, I underestimated you."

I breathed hard, wanting nothing more than to strangle him until he took his last breath.

That bastard had tried to kill all of us. Worse—he'd involved an innocent family.

"You're a traitor," I said through clenched teeth.

He straightened and calmly took a step toward me.

"You might think so," he said, "but the truth is, I'm a protector of my people. You, Silverstasia, were the threat." He sighed dramatically. "I tried to eliminate that threat. Unfortunately, it looks like you're all a bunch of cockroaches."

My gaze involuntarily shot toward his approaching men and their guns.

He wouldn't do it, would he? I thought back to the first dream I'd had when we arrived in the bunker. I'd dreamed that our people had been shot at. Had this been a premonition? Were we about to be shot at point-blank?

Without me having to give the order, everyone behind me raised their guns.

"Whoa," Jared said. "There's no need for that."

He whistled, and his men lowered their guns, though it was obvious they didn't want to. Pipes—the thick, bearded man who had been bitten by Logan's dog—stomped toward us, his oversized boots smacking against the concrete floor. He held on to his bandaged hand and glared at me as if I were responsible for the bite.

"There's no need for violence," Jared said.

"A bit late for that," I said. "You tried to have us killed."

"I did," he admitted plainly. "But I failed."

"So you think all is forgiven?" I said.

This man was a lunatic. He was even worse than the Elites I'd met. How could he outright admit to trying to kill us yet behave as if it was no big deal? As if I was supposed to simply forget about it and move on with my life?

"You don't have to forgive me," he said. "But I would like to be able to put this behind us."

Was he out of his mind? I wasn't ready to let this go. And how could I trust him after what he'd done? How could I be certain he wouldn't kill me in my sleep?

"What did you tell the others inside the bunker?" I asked.

Jared shrugged as if the story wasn't even worth mentioning. "I told them we got separated when a few stray wild ones—"

"Woodfaces," Pipes corrected.

Jared rolled his eyes at the sound of their name. "When a few Woodfaces," he corrected, "attacked."

His lips pulled up on one side, and a snaggletooth made an appearance. "I mean, you did say you were attacked by one of those savages a few days ago, didn't you? So it's perfectly plausible that more were waiting out there."

"Well, that's a lie," I said. "We weren't separated and you know it. You took off, hoping I'd chase after you so that we'd fall right into your trap. And Elias deserves to know the truth. Everyone does."

I couldn't believe how easily the words were spilling out of my mouth. But I didn't care. Confrontation didn't bother me, especially when it involved right from wrong.

And he was wrong. What he'd done was absolutely wrong.

I took another step, prepared to walk right past him and enter the bunker, when he stuck out his arm and blocked me from going any farther.

"Let me make something perfectly clear to you, Silver." He lowered his voice. "You were supposed to die out there."

I grinded my teeth until they squeaked.

"But you didn't. And now, we have to coexist once more."

"No, we don't," I threatened.

His features softened, as if he were amused by my anger. "But *we do*," he said. "You see, Elias doesn't tolerate violence within these walls, or outside of them, for that matter. So you don't have to worry about me or my men hurting you in here. What you do have to worry about is everyone else... You know, if the people start dividing again."

What was he even talking about?

"You see," he continued, "I have more followers than you realize. If you go in there and open that pretty little mouth of yours, half the citizens will believe you, and the other half will stand by me. Do you really want to cause a war?"

I stared at him, and then at his men. How was I supposed to respond to that? Of course, I didn't want a war. But what else was I supposed to do? He *had* tried to kill us. People deserved to know that.

Suddenly, I thought back to Lutum and how often people lied to get themselves out of trouble with the Defenders. Whether it had to do with stealing additional food, or stepping on forbidden territory—people often lied to avoid trouble.

Was Jared asking me to lie?

How could I do that? Grandma had always told me to speak the truth.

"Think it over," Jared said. He lowered his arm and jerked his head sideways, ordering his men to step aside and line up against the wall.

"Why did you destroy the ramps?" I asked.

Jared scratched at his bristly chin. "A precaution. In case you survived." He rolled his eyes. "Which you did... so that was a waste of a grenade." He eyed me from head to toe. "Looks like you had a nice swim."

"And what do you expect us to tell the people inside?" I said. "We can't get wheat anymore, thanks to you."

"Oh, you're creative," he said. "I'm sure you can build yourself another pretty little ramp."

He was so condescending about it that I wanted to punch him in the throat.

"And how do I know you won't try to kill me again?"

He looked at his men, laughed, and leaned back against the wall. "You don't. And even though you can't believe a word I say, I assure you that killing you is no longer part of my plan."

"Your plan?" I asked.

He looked smug but didn't respond. Then, he pushed himself off the wall with his boot. "Oh, no, Silverstasia. I very much want you alive for what's to come."

CHAPTER 29

When I stepped out into the courtyard, I was taken aback by the silence.

People lowered their wooden weapons, others rose from the garden beds, using their forearms to shield the sun from their eyes.

Everyone stopped what they were doing to watch us enter.

"They're alive!" someone shouted.

At once, loud voices spread throughout the courtyard and countless people ran toward us. Some cheered, others cried, but they all did the same thing—greeted us with open arms.

"Where were you?"

"What happened?"

"Are you all right?"

Everyone wanted answers.

But I'd warned my crew to keep quiet about what had happened. If they wanted to tell Jared's tale—the one about a few stray

Woodfaces attacking us—they were welcome to do so. I, on the other hand, had no intention of lying to my friends. While I wouldn't tell them the truth, I certainly didn't want to feed them a lie, either.

"Silver!" Sadie cried out.

She dropped her bow and ran toward me so fast I thought her legs might unhinge from her hips. Without slowing down, she threw her arms around my neck, making me stumble back several steps. I was surprised we didn't fall into the grass.

Dax, Rose, and Danika were next to approach with large grins on their faces.

When Sadie finally let go, she pulled away and wiped a tear from the corner of her eye. Then, she cleared her throat.

"I told you," Dax said.

Sadie rolled her eyes at her.

"I told Sadie you were fine—that you were a survivor and that you'd be back," Dax said, nudging Sadie in the ribs.

"I-I thought you were dead," Sadie said.

I felt terrible for having put her through that.

I wanted to hug her and tell her how sorry I was, but Sadie hated to get emotional. So rather than get mushy with her, I punched her shoulder and said, "Well, karma. Now you know how it feels."

She punched me back, but it made her laugh, which was what I'd been going for.

She wiped the underneath of her eye again and stared at the sky as if the sun's bright rays would dry them out quicker for her. "So, what happened? Why did Jared come back, and you didn't?" She moved closer, her voice becoming a whisper. "Did he do something?"

Lyla and Lyson came running, interrupting my chat with Sadie.

After I greeted them both, surprisingly, Lyla returned my smile. Was that what it took for her to be nice to me? For her to think I'd died?

"To be honest, I can't talk about that right now," I whispered to Sadie.

She scrunched her nose, likely about to punch my arm again. But when she caught my eyes darting from Dax, to Rose, to Danika, and everyone else around me, she shouted, "Give the girl some space!"

Before dispersing, everyone patted my back and said, "Good to have you back," or "Happy to know you're okay." When it was Rose's turn, she made some hand gestures and smiled sweetly, her brown cheeks ballooning under her eyes.

Danika wrapped a pale arm around Rose and leaned into her. "She says"—she repeated Rose's gestures slowly—"she's happy you're back."

I nodded and said, "Thank you," but Danika shook her head and made another gesture—she touched her chin, her fingers bouncing off and moving away from her face.

I repeated the gesture to Rose, and it made her smile. She went on to make another gesture, which I assumed meant *You're welcome.*

"She's been teaching me," Danika said proudly. "I can teach you, too."

"I'd like that," I said.

Danika and Rose walked away together. It was sweet to see what great friends they'd become. Dax went on to meet up with her new girlfriend, Mia, and kissed her cheek.

When everyone was gone, Sadie gave me a meaningful look that I knew meant *Spill the truth.*

But I couldn't. As much as I wanted to, I was afraid that if I told her about Jared trying to kill me, she'd go after him herself and get hurt. Either that, or she'd hurt him and a war would start.

In the distance, I heard a man ask about Westin. Judging by his height, size, and facial structure, I assumed he was Westin's father. James was quick to intervene, and although I couldn't make out what he was saying, it was obvious he was reassuring the man—likely telling him that Westin was being treated for minor wounds, which wasn't exactly a lie, but it wasn't the whole truth, either.

I supposed lies could sometimes be useful.

When the man tried to rush past James, James quickly stopped him and kept talking while making big gestures. What was he telling him? That Westin would come out on his own? The man seemed reluctant, but when someone called to him for help to lift a log, he turned away from James.

Sadie hopped sideways, using her head to block my view. "Hello?"

"Sorry," I said, returning my focus to her. "I can't tell you right now."

She pulled her face back. "Because we're outside? Let's go in—"

"No," I said. "I can't tell you at all. At least not yet. It's not because I don't want to, it's—"

She scoffed in my face. "You don't trust me."

"What? No, that's not it at all—"

"I've never given you a reason to not trust me," she said tightly. "And I would never repeat a word of what you say. I thought you knew me better than that."

"It's not that simple."

She shook her head. "It never is with you."

I was about to apologize again when she turned around and went back to the courtyard's new fighting grounds. Why was she so upset? Why couldn't she understand that I was keeping this to myself for a reason? Wasn't that better than lying to her?

It made me feel like garbage, even though it hadn't been a lie.

Just as I let out a sigh, a warm hand landed on my shoulder. I spun around to find Reina smiling at me—something she rarely did.

"Good to have you back, kiddo." She stood without moving, and I wasn't sure if I was supposed to try to hug her or say something, so I did neither.

"Many thought you were dead," she said. "Care to tell me what that was about?"

I glanced back at Sadie. If I told Reina now, it would only worsen the tension between Sadie and me.

"It's complicated," I said honestly.

"Uncomplicate it for me."

I blinked hard, trying to find my words.

"Not here," Reina said. "Come. Finn wants a word with you."

CHAPTER 30

We entered a space that looked nothing like our living quarters.

At the center sat a sleek metal desk that reflected the white light of a swaying, overhead bulb. Even the walls seemed made of metal, or at least something that resembled it. I'd never known much about metal.

There was no furniture in sight—only chairs around the table.

"What is this place?" I asked, looking around the bare space.

Finn leaned back into his chair, looking proud. "A Faraday room," he said.

"Fair day?" I repeated.

He laughed and stood up, pushing his chair out with the back of his knees. Greeting me with a firm handshake, he stared me dead in the eyes. "I'm happy you're here, Silver."

I didn't need a hug from him to know he'd been concerned. It was all over his face.

"Thanks."

"And I didn't say fair day," he said, chuckling again. "I said Faraday. It isn't exactly relevant these days anymore, but back before the war, rooms like these were used to discuss top secret missions without the risk of being heard."

"How could anyone hear us unless they're inside the room with us?" I asked.

He looked at Reina, seemingly amused by my lack of knowledge.

"There were all kinds of devices people used, Silver. Some could hear through walls and at great distances. The military couldn't risk anything like that."

That didn't make much sense to me. We were hidden underground with thick walls of stone and metal all around us.

"You'd think this bunker would keep the bad guys out," I said.

Slowly, he sat back down and pulled his chair in. "Any organization is at risk of having a spy infiltrate."

Infiltrate? What did that even mean? By the look on his face, it sounded like he was talking about bad people making their way into a group of good people, a bit like Jared.

When I didn't respond, Finn extended both arms in the air, showcasing the shiny walls. "Elias said we can use this anytime we want to have meetings. Pretty generous, isn't it?"

I wasn't sure how I felt about Elias, either. The last time we'd spoken, he'd earned my trust. But after what had happened with Jared, I couldn't help but wonder if the two brothers were working together.

Maybe this room wasn't safe at all. For all we knew, Elias was using some advanced device to listen in on us. Why else offer Finn the room for private conversations?

"Have a seat," Finn said.

It wasn't an order, but I sat down anyway. Reina stood behind me, unmoving.

"You're safe here, Silver," Finn said, leaning forward. His beard had grown quite a bit since we'd arrived here, but it suited him. "You can tell us what happened if you feel comfortable. If you don't, that's okay. I just hope that if we're in any kind of danger—if you ran into any new tribes that could pose a threat—"

"I didn't," I said at once.

This hadn't been a lie. The tribe I'd met posed no threat to us and the last thing I wanted was for Jared to somehow find out about Lockridge.

Tapping his foot against the metal floor, he stared up at Reina as if trying to hold back an entire conversation from spilling out of his mouth. He wanted to know what had happened, but he didn't want to come across as demanding or pushy.

"Something happened," I admitted.

He leaned in without a word.

"But I can't talk about it."

He parted his lips, but nothing came out. Then, he ran a hand through his caramel-brown hair and held it there, waiting. When I still didn't say a word, he returned both hands to the table and sighed.

"Well, are you all right?" he asked. "Did something traumatic—"

I shook my head. Although it *had* been traumatic, I was used to violence—I'd grown up in Lutum. But I got the sense that wasn't what he'd meant when he said traumatic. Maybe he thought someone had sexually abused me. Grandma had warned me about this at an early age, telling me never to trust any Defender, no matter how friendly they seemed. She said some of them sometimes pretended to be nice to girls coming of age, only to later have their way with them.

I still wasn't sure what that meant, exactly, but Grandma's frown had been enough to scare me.

"I'm okay," I said. "But something did happen. Something I want to tell you. But I can't."

This seemed to confuse him, and although I couldn't see Reina behind me, I imagined her features mirrored those of Finn's.

I swallowed hard, afraid he might let go of his kindness as Mr. Darwin had done and demand that I give him answers.

Locking his fingers together over the table, Finn breathed out slowly. "All right."

"All right?" I repeated.

It couldn't be so simple. Sadie had grown visibly upset when I denied her the truth. How could the leader of our people be so nonchalant about the whole thing?

"I understand," he said. "I trust your judgment, Silver. I also trust that if you *feel* we should know anything, you'll tell us."

I paused. "Well, there is *something*."

"I'm listening," he said.

"The ramp on the other side of the river was destroyed. We can't collect wheat until it's fixed."

He didn't raise his brows or twist his features. He simply nodded. "Thank you for telling us. We can provide you with all the materials you need." He hesitated. "Of course, unless you no longer want to go outside—"

"I still want to go."

I wanted to add, "As long as Jared doesn't come with us," but I got the feeling that Jared didn't plan on following us anymore. He was up to something else. Besides, he'd also made it sound like he had no intention of killing me.

Finn crossed his fingers and smiled sweetly at me. "Thank you for sharing this information with me. Is there anything else?"

I nodded.

He released his clasped fingers and stretched them out as if to say, *I'm listening.*

I looked around the room, panicking.

"No one is listening," he said. "But if you're afraid they are, you can whisper it to me."

Slowly, I pushed my chair back, and it rattled over the tiny grooves on the metal floor. I made my way around the table, took in a deep breath, and leaned into Finn's ear.

"Jared is very dangerous," was all I said.

When I pulled away, Finn didn't look surprised at all.

"I know," he said, "but thank you for confirming my thoughts."

"You knew?" I said.

"I don't know what happened," he admitted, "and you're entitled to keep that information to yourself. But I do know *something* happened. And I do know *someone* was involved. I've met many people like him in my lifetime."

"So what do we do now?" I asked.

He and Reina shared a quiet, meaningful look.

"We're working on it," Reina said.

CHAPTER 31

As the days went on, tension grew.

Most Undergrounders seemed satisfied with the answer they'd been given by James and the other crew members who had nearly died in the fire with me. It was an easy story to swallow: we'd been attacked by a few enemies, and now, those enemies were dead.

Elias had also arranged for a team of builders to rebuild the river's bridge. He said this would grant us easy access to the wheat and also allow us to retrieve the abandoned rover. I wasn't sure if they'd started building yet, but I liked the idea.

The problems were mostly solved, and everything was back to normal.

But for Sadie, the problems were far from being solved. She knew me enough to know that the story wasn't true. Every time she asked me to confirm it, I told her I couldn't.

By the time the weekend came around, I'd

grown so tired of having to defend my position that I withdrew into the library, wanting to be alone. It was the first time I'd ever set foot in a library, and the moment I did, I forgot all about the fire, Sadie's anger toward me, and Jared.

I stared in awe at the countless wooden shelves full of colorful book spines. The shelves were endless, running along numerous walls. Some were so tall that they nearly reached the ceiling. I wondered how anyone could reach that high to grab a book.

The place was huge. If I wasn't careful, I'd easily get lost and forget how to return to the main entrance.

Gazing around in awe, I breathed in, filling my nose with the scent of lemon and lavender. Everything looked so clean, and shiny.

A dark beige carpet ran along the floor, and atop it were large green arrows pointing in one direction. Was I supposed to follow them? Not knowing what else to do, I followed their direction.

They led me to a booth with a middle-aged woman sitting behind a sheet of glass. She rested her cheek on one tight fist, focusing on something in front of her. As I approached, she didn't look up at me. It wasn't until I tapped on the glass that she jolted upright, a red fist imprint on her cheek.

"Oh, hi there!" She smacked her book

closed. "I'm so sorry. I was reading the documentary on Kormace Island. Can you believe what those women went through? Having to live on an islánd like that?"

I hadn't the slightest clue what she was talking about, so I nodded politely.

"The green arrows led me here," I said.

"What's your name, honey? And your room number?"

"Um, Silver—Silverstasia Blackwood. Room H101."

"Like the 101 Dalmatians!" she said merrily.

I couldn't help but smile. At least someone else thought the same way I did.

Suddenly, a furry creature jumped onto the woman's lap and I took a step backward.

"Oh, don't you worry about Mr. Hufflepuff here," she said. "He's the sweetest thing."

"Is that a cat?" I asked.

I'd never seen one before. At least, not in person. It had pointed ears, a pointed nose, and long white whiskers that looked thin and sharp enough to tickle skin. It was more colorful than what I imagined a cat looking like—full of grays, browns, whites, and even a pink nose.

The woman—whose name tag read *Mary*—alternated scratching the creature's fuzzy chin and head. "Sure is. First time you see one?"

I nodded.

"Want to pet him?" she asked.

I shook my head. As much as I loved animals, I felt intimidated by them. Maybe after I'd seen a few more cats, I'd get the courage to pet one.

"I bet you haven't pet the dogs yet, either, have ya, sweetheart?"

"No, I haven't," I said.

Although I'd had several opportunities in the courtyard, I'd never touched one. They seemed soft and friendly, but every time they *panted*—a term Sadie had taught me—their sharp teeth reminded me of the wolves that had nearly killed me and I wanted to turn the other way.

Maz kept her bloodhounds and pit bulls on the training side of the courtyard, away from the children. She said she didn't want them becoming soft or growing too accustomed to affection. On the other side of the courtyard, where children often played, were other breeds I'd learned about during my training days.

There were German shepherds, golden retrievers, and Labradors. Most of them roamed around freely, greeting people with wagging tails and big pink tongues, while others wore harnesses and followed only a single person around.

Sadie told me those dogs were referred to as *service dogs* and helped people with various conditions or ailments. Their vests were reflective, and when children ran up to them, parents were quick to pull them away. At first, I thought they were vicious, but I quickly learned that like Maz's dogs, they needed to remain focused on their training.

Mary knocked on the glass between us, and I jolted out of my daze.

"Your card, sweetheart."

She slid it toward me on the table. "What's this?" I asked.

"A library card, love. Any time you want to take a book out, go to one of those booths over there. Then scan both your card and the back of the book."

"Take a book out?" I asked.

"Out of the library, silly," she said. "We need to keep track of where all our books are going."

It made sense. I thanked her and grabbed my new card, which felt silky and hard. I ran my finger across the smooth texture, noting that my name was written in black solid letters across the bottom: Silverstasia Blackwood.

It made me grin broadly, and for a moment, I wanted to run home and tell Grandma all about my very first library card. Just as my throat swelled, someone poked my shoulder and I twirled around, swallowing my sadness.

Lyson stood with three books clutched to his chest, his chin pressed against the largest one. "You found the library," he said.

I lowered my card and forced a smile. "I did. Is it as nice as the one in Ortus?"

He tightened his grip around his books and stared at the high ceilings, his lip curving upward on one side. "I never thought I'd say this, but this place is way nicer."

I wasn't surprised to hear it. I couldn't imagine any place being nicer than this one. It was so vast and open.

"I'll show you my favorite spot if you want," he said.

When I nodded, he led me down another beige-carpeted hallway, a set of stairs, and another set of giant, white-tiled stairs that descended farther underground. As we went down, I slid my hand along the railing.

This place is huge, I thought to myself.

"It has to be big," Lyson said as if reading my mind. "The world's knowledge is in here."

"How?" I asked.

He shrugged. "I don't know. Elias says his father told him these books were already here when they found the bunker."

"I thought the army owned this place," I said.

"They did," Lyson said, "but we don't know who else lived here before us. There's a lot we don't know."

My mouth agape, I took it all in, excited to

start scavenging through the books.

Once we reached the bottom of the stairs, we turned to the right and walked next to the staircase by a smooth wooden wall full of brown swirls. I was surprised when Lyson took another sharp turn and brought us *under* the staircase.

I never expected the underneath of a staircase to look like this. Although I could see the steps above, they were high up and didn't make the space feel cramped at all. Several circular lights ran along both sides of the wall—some were on, others, off. At the very back, where the space became narrower and darker, was a couch next to an unlit lamp.

"That's my spot," he said.

"You own it?"

He smiled at me, staring longer than necessary. "No one owns any space in here." The words came out like he was holding back a laugh. "It's just a saying. I mean it's my favorite spot, and I come here all the time. You're welcome to use it whenever you'd like, even if I'm here."

He stared at me again, and I grew uncomfortable.

Why was he looking at me like that? No one stared *that* long.

"What are you doing?" I asked.

This took him aback.

"What do you mean?" he said.

I scrunched my nose. "Why are you staring at me like that?"

"Oh, um—" he stammered. "I'm sorry. I didn't realize I was doing it. You're, um, you're very pretty, Silver, and sometimes I can't help but look at you."

I became even more uncomfortable. Was he expecting me to say something back? To tell him he was pretty, too? Was that the polite thing to do?

"Um, you're pretty too," I said, feeling stupid.

He chuckled, still watching me.

"Why does your sister hate me so much?" I said to change the topic.

The amused look on his face vanished and his features hardened. "Lyla? She doesn't hate you. Why would you say that?"

"She's always rude to me," I said. "If I've done something—"

He shook his head. "You haven't done anything, Silver." He went on to bite his lower lip as if trying to determine whether or not to share a secret.

"You remind her of her best friend," he finally said. "I personally don't see the resemblance, but Lyla's made a point of telling me several times how much you look like her, and I think that hurts her."

"Why would it hurt her?" I asked. "And what friend? Lyla always seems to be alone."

"Tia," he said as if I'd recognize her name. Sighing, he walked over to the sofa and I followed him. He sat down with a plop and rested his elbows on his long thighs. "A few years ago, Finn went through a severe depression. No one talks about it anymore, but it was pretty bad. Around the same time, a guy named Bacchus discovered something we later found out was a poppy—a flower that contains seeds full of something. A painkiller. I think it's called morphine. Anyway, he found it near the river, growing in dirt and sand. The guy was a huge experimenter, always making new brews of teas or mixing different spices. Well, he used the poppy to make a tea, and it gave him one heck of a buzz."

A *buzz*, I remembered, apparently made people feel funny after drinking alcohol.

"But this wasn't a regular buzz," he said. "It was intense and made him want to keep doing it. Eventually, his friends found out about it, including Tia, who was struggling with depression herself. I guess it helped her with it."

"With her depression?" I asked.

"Yeah." He nodded. "It had some sort of numbing effect. I mean, which is great, because our medics started using it later once the truth came out."

He looked heartbroken as he told the story. Why was he so sad? If something could cure depression, wasn't that a good thing?

"So did Finn take some?" I asked.

Lyson looked at me intently. "No, of course not. He didn't even know it was being circulated, and if he had, he would have put a stop to it... maybe even saved a bunch of lives."

I swallowed hard. What did he mean by that, *saved*? Had people died? I didn't say anything.

"Bacchus was the first to die. His dad found him in his bed, cold and stiff."

I swallowed even harder. I'd seen people get beaten—even incinerated by the Defenders—but I couldn't imagine finding a loved one's dead body somewhere. It made me sick to my stomach.

"More and more kids died afterward, too," he said. "And then, Tia died." He paused. "My sister's the one who found her near the river, lying on her back and staring up at the sky."

I was too stunned to say anything, so I sat in silence, looking at the tips of my boots.

"People thought that maybe the poppies had poisoned them or something," he went on. "But a few medics came forward and explained something called an overdose."

I'd heard the term before, but only because

Grandma had spoken of an epidemic back in her day. She said that something called fentanyl was going around, killing thousands of young people. I still didn't understand why anyone would take something so dangerous, especially knowing that others were dying from it.

Lyson's eyes glazed over as he no doubt replayed those awful memories in his mind. I wondered how many friends he'd lost to these overdoses.

"Why did others keep taking it after Bacchus died?" I asked.

Lyson scoffed. "I kept asking myself the same thing. But this stuff... these poppies. It turned people into zombies. Some of them even went mad if they didn't get more. My aunt said it was called addiction. I didn't understand it at the time, but now I do. They couldn't stop. I mean, imagine being able to take away all your pain and feeling nothing but absolute ecstasy. Wouldn't it be hard to come back to the real world?"

I pondered this for a moment. "Yeah, it would be, but I'd do it if I had people who cared about me. I wouldn't want to hurt those people."

Lyson smirked, and it made me feel like I still wasn't *getting* it.

"It's not that simple," he said. He paused

again, his gaze stuck on the carpet at our feet. What wasn't he telling me?

Finally, he sighed. "After Tia died, Lyla got into drinking the tea."

I could tell the memory still haunted him.

"She changed," he said. "She wasn't even herself anymore. That tea... whatever it was, it turned her into someone else. Almost like something had possessed her. No matter how hard I tried to get her to stop, she wouldn't."

I swallowed hard, imagining how difficult that must have been for him.

He ran a hand through his bright blond hair, leaned back into the sofa, and stared at the stone steps above our heads. "I almost lost her."

We sat in silence for a moment, a heavy weight pressing on my chest.

"What happened after?" I asked.

"When teens starting dying, it pulled Finn out of his depression and he got involved," he said. "I owe him everything."

"He stopped her?" I asked.

Lyson scoffed. "You could say that. It was a whole ordeal. She had to be tied down to a bed in the hospital and monitored until she got better. They were giving her something, too. She was so sick... so pale. She wasn't the only one. Adults stepped in and put regulations around the growth of poppies. We had actual guards watching the flowers day and night. It caused fights because parents who lost their children wanted the flowers destroyed, but medics wanted to use them for medicinal purposes. They said if the dosage was controlled, these poppies could change everything. So we kept them. We just didn't let anyone cultivate them unless it was for the hospital."

I parted my lips to ask him how long it took for Lyla to return to normal, but he continued, "She was in the hospital for weeks, *detoxing*, as they called it." He breathed out hard. "Listen, I'm sorry if she's been giving you a hard time. I think you're just triggering memories for her. It might look like we've had an easy life, Lyla and I. I mean, we aren't from Lutum, so we really shouldn't complain. But our mother died while giving birth to us, and our father died when we were only ten. That messed Lyla up a lot, I think."

"I-I'm so sorry," I said.

I thought back to Mother and how cruel she'd been to me. Looking back, I knew she'd been miserable. She hated her life, and she somehow blamed me for it. Maybe she thought that if she hadn't had a child, she might have had a better chance at winning the lottery and joining the Elites. But none of that mattered anymore. At least I'd had a mother, and even better, I'd had a loving grandmother who took great care of me.

I was one of the lucky ones.

Suddenly, he patted my knee, jolted upright, and beamed. "Enough of this dark talk. How about we go find you some books?"

CHAPTER 32

I lay in bed most of the night, reading a new book I'd found.

It was about spirituality, something I'd never had the opportunity to read about. In Lutum, books like this were nonexistent. But now that I no longer lived in Lutum, I figured it was time to start exploring the world's ancient beliefs and religions.

It brought me comfort to know that so many people believed in life after death. Although hard to fathom, I held on to it because it made me feel closer to Grandma. And even if it wasn't true, the comfort felt real, so I kept reading.

A knock on my door shook me out of my bubble. I glanced over my book, hoping whoever had knocked might simply go away if I didn't answer. But when a second knock came, I knew they weren't going away.

So I got up, wrapped my sheet around my

body for warmth, and made my way to the door. When I opened it, Sadie's face appeared in the crack. She looked sad—almost apologetic. She wore a white nightgown, and her hair sat in a ponytail over one shoulder. It was a soft, angelic look that didn't suit her personality.

But it was nice.

"Hey," she said.

"Hi," I said back.

"I know it's late," she said. "I didn't mean to bother you. But I saw you come back from the library early, and well"—she shot a glance at the book in my hand and the corner of her mouth turned up—"I figured you'd be up a while."

She knew me well.

"Listen, I'm sorry about earlier," she said. "I didn't mean to get upset with you hiding the truth."

"I wasn't trying to hide anything—"

"I know," she said. "Let me finish." When I didn't cut her off, she continued. "You have every right to your privacy. I guess it hurt because I thought we were close friends. But I trust you, Silver, and if you aren't telling me something, it's because you'd be risking more by telling me."

I didn't say anything, even though she was right.

"That's all," she said. "I wanted to

apologize."

She turned around, prepared to leave.

"Wait," I said. When she looked back at me, I placed my book down on the foot of my bed. "Why don't you spend the night?"

She shot a glance at the floor next to my bed.

"Not on the floor," I said, on the verge of laughing.

She pointed at the bed and raised an eyebrow.

"Yeah, on the bed," I said. "I had a difficult day, and it would be nice to not feel alone right now."

She stared at me the way Lyson had, but it didn't bother me. If anything, I liked it.

Finally, she nodded, stepped inside, and joined me at the bed. She climbed in first, awkwardly bunching some of the blanket up to her chest. I climbed in next to her, then reached for the lamp and turned out the lights.

We lay in the dark without a word, our shoulders pressed up against each other.

Her warmth calmed me, even if only against my arm. It made me feel whole, and protected, and even vulnerable.

"Are you okay?" she whispered in the dark.

Then, as if her words alone had been enough to trigger my emotions, my throat swelled. I thought of Jared's threats, of Lyson's story, of Mother, and Grandma. I was beyond exhausted, and the more I thought of everything, the more I wanted to cry. I hated feeling emotional.

I didn't answer.

I was afraid that if I opened my mouth to respond, I'd start crying. So instead, I nodded in the dark, not realizing she couldn't see me.

"Silver?" she asked.

When I still didn't respond, she shifted in the bed and laid a warm hand over my chest.

Suddenly, everything came out, and I found myself bawling harder than I'd ever cried before. Although I'd managed to get through the days, the truth was, I was terrified and heartbroken. I'd lost my family, and there was no telling what the future held for us.

"Come here," she whispered.

She slid an arm under my neck and pulled me in against her. It was the warmest touch I'd ever felt. She breathed against the top of my head, holding me tight, and we lay in silence as I cried until my head hurt.

When I finally stopped, my nose was so stuffy I could barely breathe. I was sure I'd drooled on her nightgown.

"I-I'm sorry," I mumbled.

"Don't be sorry," she said. "This world is a difficult place, and you've been through so much."

I didn't know how to respond. Everyone had been through a lot. Did they cry like this, too? Or were they stronger than me?

As if reading my mind, she said, "Crying doesn't make you weak. It takes strength to let your feelings out."

I found that hard to believe coming from Sadie. She was the strongest person I knew, which made me feel even more embarrassed for having cried in her arms like that.

"Want to know a secret?" she asked.

I nodded against her chest.

"I cry almost every night."

I pulled my face back, seeing only her dark silhouette. "What? Why?"

She shrugged, her blanket making a chafing sound. "Because life's hard, Silver. I miss people I've lost. I'm still sad that we lost Penelope. I miss my parents, even though I was young when I lost them." She paused. "And I'm terrified of losing you."

I held on to those words for several seconds, appreciating the weight of them. Without a word, I pressed my forehead back against her chest and breathed out hard.

"I... Me too," I said.

I lay in her warm embrace until colorful images swirled in my mind and I fell asleep.

As the next morning unfolded, I didn't give much thought to Jared or how he'd tried to kill me.

Waking up next to Sadie made me feel content and whole. All I wanted was to enjoy my day and forget the bad. We ate breakfast as we did every other morning, only this time, everything seemed *better*.

I wasn't sure if it was because of the moment I'd shared with Sadie, or the book I'd started reading, but I was certainly feeling better.

Our friends joined us at the breakfast table—Rose, Danika, Dax, and her new girlfriend, Mia. Even Hudson, who no longer had the sling around his arm, sat next to Sadie. We laughed and talked about events happening in the courtyard.

Apparently, something called Halloween was approaching, and in the bunker, this was a popular event. Mia explained to us that on the thirty-first of October, everyone was to dress up in a costume. There would be a celebration, as well as honey and maple candy handed out to the children.

It sounded magical, and I couldn't wait to start thinking about what costume I'd wear.

"You can work with the seamstresses in the courtyard for a costume," Mia said. "If you're lucky, they'll create something for you. Otherwise, we recycle a lot of our costumes and alter the sizes for different people."

Hudson smacked his hand on the table. "I'm gonna be a gorilla."

Everyone laughed.

"Where the hell will you get the supplies to make that?" Sadie asked.

Hudson shrugged his square shoulders. "Coconut hair."

Again, everyone laughed, and a few others started talking about what they planned to be.

Rose then gestured something and everyone went quiet to watch her.

"Rose says she wants to be a cactus," Danika said, trying not to burst out laughing.

I scrunched my nose. "Why a cactus?" I asked her.

Rose beamed and gestured some more.

Danika smiled, watching her. "Her favorite plant."

"Hey, nothing wrong with that," Mia said. "That's what's fun about all of this. You get to use your imagination and be whatever you want to be."

We laughed some more as we got up and cleared our plates from the tables. When we went outside, a bright morning sun and a clear blue sky greeted us.

"How do you feel about ax throwing?" Sadie

asked, smirking at me.

Was she being serious? Would I get to learn a new weapon?

"That, or crossbow," she said. "Reina gave us a few from Elias's supply. She said she wants us to perfect our crossbow skills."

As much as I wanted to learn how to throw an ax, I needed to get better at firing a crossbow.

"Let's do crossbow," I said.

The group broke apart as everyone went on to their chores. Danika left and walked toward the daycare, and I was happy to see she was getting to work with children again. As she jogged through the luscious green grass, a young man met her halfway, locking hands with her. She leaned into his chest and kissed his neck.

It made me happy to see my friends happy.

Sadie and I headed to the training grounds, where Maz ran in circles with her dogs at the far back, training them to run over and under obstacles.

As I approached, several heads turned my way.

I was getting tired of people staring at me.

I turned to Sadie, prepared to say something, when I noticed she wasn't even looking at me; she was looking *beyond* me.

What was everyone so fascinated with?

Before I could even turn around, Dax, Danika, and Rose came stampeding toward us, their mouths agape and their arms waving above their heads.

I spun around—Asako.

She stood with her eyes squinted so tightly it looked like they were shut. Next to her stood a woman clad in a light blue uniform, a matching hat, and a little red cross on her chest. Was this what the Undergrounder medics wore? I'd never seen a medic in uniform here. Elias had told me the hospital wing resided farther inside the bunker, where most civilians steered clear.

"Asako!" Dax shouted, running up to her.

But as she drew in close, the medic stuck out a stiff arm and said, "Whoa, easy."

At the same time, Asako retreated behind the nurse like a frightened animal. She curled her lips above her small, yellow teeth and grimaced at the sky as if the sun were hurting her face.

What was wrong with her? What had the Woodfaces done?

"She's in rehabilitation," the medic said.

I took a step forward, but the medic's big brown eyes warned me not to take another.

"This is her first time outside in weeks," the medic said. "She's been working closely with a psychologist—"

"A psycho-what?" Dax said.

I nudged her in the ribs. "A head doctor."

Dax tightened her lips and nodded.

"So, if you wouldn't mind—" the medic said.

She seemed impatient, likely because she wanted what was best for Asako, and we were getting in the way of that.

"G-good to have you back," Danika said awkwardly.

Asako snapped her head even farther away, her dark hair covering most of her face.

As she walked through the courtyard alongside the medic, she observed everyone from a distance. She moved with a slouched posture, and every few seconds, hurled herself against the nurse, clutching her blue clothes for dear life.

"What happened to her?" Sadie asked.

Everyone eyed each other, likely wondering the same thing. Although we had no idea what she'd been through, it was apparent the Woodfaces had put her through hell.

CHAPTER 33

"Focus," Sadie said.

It was hard to focus after seeing Asako like that. I wanted to talk to her and ask her what had happened. But I knew there was a reason I hadn't seen her in weeks. She'd been kept away from civilization to heal. I had to trust that the medics here knew what they were doing and would continue to work with her until she was back to normal, or at least, somewhat normal.

When I wasn't thinking of Asako, I thought of Westin, hoping that Elias would get the ramp fixed in time for us to return to Lockridge to get him. How would we explain that, anyway? James and the others had spun a story about him being in the bunker's medical unit, but that wasn't true, and if the medical staff got around to hearing that, they'd quickly expose the lie.

Every few seconds, I considered peeking behind the wooden wall separating us from the rest of the courtyard. I wanted to ensure that Westin's father didn't walk up to Asako's medic, requesting an update on his son.

"You've missed every single shot," Sadie growled.

She tore my bolts out from large planks of rotting wood behind the targets.

I lowered my crossbow, sighing. "Sorry. I have a lot on my mind."

"I get it," she said. "Your friend looks like she's been abused, or tortured." She bit her lip and stopped talking, likely sensing that I wasn't in the mood to receive a visual of the torment they'd put her through. "I mean, it looks like she's been through a lot."

I began to imagine all the horrendous things they could have done to her, when Sadie handed me back my bolts. "Load up. Take another shot."

It was a welcome distraction, so I loaded my weapon and fired again. This time, I hit the corner of the target.

"Better," she said. "Your target wouldn't be dead, but it would give you time to run."

I loaded another bolt.

"Hello?" she said. "Nothing?"

"Huh?" I said, bent forward as I cocked the crossbow.

"You missed the punchline entirely," she said.

"What punchline?" I asked.

"I just said it would give you time to *run*."

I didn't see what was so funny about that.

"You know, because you suck so much at fighting lately that you'd have better odds if you ran."

I rolled my eyes. This time, I wanted to prove her wrong, so I breathed in deeply, then held my breath and took aim.

Snap.

The bolt pierced through the center of the target.

She smacked her hands together. "Is that all it takes? For me to insult you?"

I laughed. "I prefer using a bow or a spear."

"Why?" she said. "This thing is pretty badass." She moved toward me and grabbed the crossbow. Without hesitating, she loaded it quickly, raised it, and fired a shot. The bolt hit the target dead center, pushing my bolt aside.

"Yeah, that's great," I said. "Now what do you do if someone's running at you? It'll take you a few seconds to—"

She jolted back up, the crossbow already loaded. "You were saying?"

I rolled my eyes. "Regular bows are still faster."

"They are," she said. "But every weapon has its advantage. If we're fighting against armed soldiers, say, like the Woodfaces. Well, I'd much prefer using this bad boy over a regular old bow. Better accuracy and more power. It would probably tear through their stupid wooden chest plates."

I thought back to the Woodface who had grabbed me in the wheat field and my heart started pounding hard. What if he hadn't been the last one? What if there were more? Suddenly, everything around me began to spin, and I nearly tumbled over.

"Hey," came Sadie's voice.

She gripped my shoulders and gave me a firm shake. "You okay?"

I wanted to tell her everything. I was so tired of hiding this secret from her. When we locked eyes, I knew I couldn't hold it in any longer. "There's something I want to tell you."

Just then, voices erupted in the distance and Elias came out cheering with Finn and Reina at his side. Around them were a few other people, clapping and dancing and singing a tune I'd heard a few times in Ortus.

Was that the birthday song?

Elias seemed to be having the most fun of all. He smacked his feet into the grass as he spun in circles, singing deeply. Little children ran up, joining in on the celebration, and one by one, more people emerged from the bunker.

Whose birthday was it?

Arahm came out next with a cart full of

cakes and cupcakes, decorated in brilliant colors that made them look delicious. His children clapped and danced around Elias, chanting with him.

It was such a sight to see that I found myself smiling and wanting to join the celebration, even though I had no idea what it was about.

"What's going on?" Sadie asked.

I shook my head. I had no idea.

We walked closer, exiting the training grounds, when Sadie's friend Elliot came running toward her, dancing like a lunatic. He was obviously trying to get us to laugh and it worked. Today, he wore blue powder over his eyelids and a golden necklace that hung over his chest. He always made an effort to look radiant, even when everyone around him wore rags to work in the gardens.

But he didn't seem to mind getting his pretty clothes dirty.

"Didn't you hear, darling?" he asked. "It's Fort Denton's thirtieth anniversary."

Sadie cocked an eyebrow at me, and I did the same. I hadn't heard anything about it. Then again, I'd been so preoccupied thinking about Jared, Lockridge, the Elites, and more, that I hadn't been paying much attention to what was going on around me.

I was surprised to see people exit the

bunker with canes and medical equipment. Even some of our people who were still healing had taken the time to come out and celebrate.

Musicians showed up with skin drums, and everyone stopped working.

All that mattered was that we came together and celebrated.

I watched as Elias grabbed a little girl by the hand and started dancing with her near the garden beds. Her smile was so big it took up half her face, and her big blue eyes gleamed with excitement as she twirled around him in a little pink dress. It was the most precious thing I'd ever seen.

Children formed a line next to Arahm's cart, waiting patiently for a piece of dessert.

"Want a cupcake?" Sadie asked, nudging me.

I warmed inwardly at the thought, but my smile vanished in an instant when I spotted the one person I hoped wouldn't be attending the celebration.

Jared.

He stood at the courtyard's entrance, leaning against the open doorway. He watched me, looking amused, but in a bad way. While everyone else was having a grand time dancing and cheering, Jared seemed to be preparing for something else.

He bowed his head slightly, shadows

deepening the bags under his eyes.

"Silver?" Sadie asked.

When I didn't budge, her gaze followed mine. "He did something to you, didn't he?" she said.

I was too angry to respond. Instead, we stood quietly, staring at each other until Jared stuck his nose up, backed up, and slid the bunker's large metal door closed.

My mouth went dry. Why was he closing it? No one ever closed that door—not unless it was nighttime and everyone was inside.

Something was wrong.

One of the guards standing next to the door left his position and reached for the handle. He tugged, over and over again, then started pounding his fists against the metal.

"J-Jared!" the guard shouted. "What are you doing? Open the door! We had a deal! We had a deal!"

His voice was so loud that the cheering in the courtyard came to an abrupt stop.

Elias swung around with a scowl on his face and marched toward the closed door. "What is the meaning of this?"

I ran, joining him at the entrance.

"I'm sorry, brother," came Jared's voice.

It was barely audible, but I was close enough to make it out.

Elias pounded on the door, creating a loud

thumping sound. "Open the door!"

"You and your people are deluded, brother," Jared said. "You won't survive more than another year like this."

Elias pounded again, and as he did so, worried faces approached the scene.

People looked at each other with large round eyes and slanted brows. Everyone looked terrified, likely wondering why Jared would have locked everyone out of the bunker.

"Brother!" Elias growled, his voice a deep rumble. It carried throughout the entire courtyard, and children began to cry.

One young boy even dropped his cupcake onto his bare toes, the blue icing staining them, and cried so hard his father had to scoop him up and rock him.

Elias turned to Sofia, who stood next to him with a hand hovering over her holstered gun.

"Do you have the keys?" Elias asked.

"I do," she said. She reached for a set of keys on her belt and picked out a large bronze key.

Elias took it from her, stuck it into the door's keyhole, and turned. Although it made an unlocking sound, the door didn't budge. Elias jammed his shoulder into the door, trying to pry it open.

Nothing.

"I-I-I," stuttered the guard standing next to him—the same guard who'd pleaded with Jared to let him in and who'd spoken about some deal.

Elias watched him.

"I–I'm so sorry," the man blurted. "I didn't… I didn't think he would do this."

"Do what?" Elias growled.

"I–I didn't know!" The man dropped to his knees and started sobbing in his hands.

Reina looked at me, clicked her fingers, and pointed behind me. At once, Sadie spun around and started ordering everyone to arm up. This only caused more panic. Those who didn't know how to fight began to cower at the opposite end of the courtyard. Parents tried to console their children, while couples and friends held on to each other tightly.

A few others simply watched, trying to make sense of what was going on.

This will all blow over shortly, they probably thought.

But I knew better.

This was what Jared had been planning. He wasn't angry with me. He was angry with Elias and all of his followers.

I ran with Sadie into the fighting grounds.

"Grab a weapon and get ready to fight!" I shouted.

I wasn't even sure why we were getting ready to fight. How could we possibly fight if we were locked out of the bunker?

But just as we were arming up, a familiar whistling sound came from above.

I searched the sky, my stomach knotting as a dozen fire arrows came flying over the wall and down toward our people.

"Arrows!" someone shouted.

Everyone dove in various directions, trying to avoid the balls of fire. One young man wasn't so lucky, and the moment the arrow made impact with his shin, his entire leg lit up. He ran in circles, trying to stop the flames, but it was no use. The fire quickly climbed up his leg and around his torso and almost consumed him entirely before two gardeners came running toward him with a bucket of water.

More arrows came down and people screamed, running like ants from a destroyed colony.

Who was attacking us? These arrows didn't belong to Jared—his men used guns.

I stared at the arrows as they landed in the stables and pierced the training ground's new wall. That fletching... I recognized it. These arrows belonged to the Woodfaces. But how was that possible? Elias had ordered the army to be destroyed.

I glanced back at the sobbing man as Elias shook him hard and raised a fist next to his face, prepared to bash him if he didn't speak. This man had done something... but what?

Suddenly, one of our stables blew up in flames and more people started screaming.

"Open the gates!" I shouted.

I wasn't even sure why I thought I had the authority to make a call like this, but I felt it was the only chance we had. If we sat in here, we would all be killed—either by our enemies' arrows, their fire, or simply through depopulation. And if we allowed them to take out half of our fighters from over the wall, we'd never stand a chance against them after that.

I had no idea what kind of numbers they had, but it didn't matter.

We had to try.

Sofia suddenly appeared next to me, carrying a large rifle. Beside her were another dozen fighters with automatic guns. She nodded at me as a way of saying, *We're here with you*, which brought me great comfort.

Two fighters dressed in black ran for the locks and chains at the center of the gates. They untied everything and pried the doors apart, running backward as the gates opened up.

I stood strong with my crossbow aimed straight ahead, prepared to kill the first person in sight.

The second the gates opened even slightly, Woodfaces began spilling their way inside, jabbing sharp weapons over their heads and crying out so wildly that chills ran down my back.

For a moment, I froze as dozens upon dozens of Woodfaces entered.

But it wasn't their numbers that frightened me.

It was the leader—a large man with a wooden mask whose posture I recognized. He was the same man who'd stood behind Asako the day they came to threaten the bunker.

This wasn't a new army at all.

Jared had somehow crossed his brother and allowed our enemies to live.

Sound faded around me as I stared at this large man—his wooden shoulder plates, the red feathers sticking straight up from his carved mask, and the massive battle-ax he held in his right hand.

Although I couldn't see his eyes through his mask, it felt like he was looking right at me.

Suddenly, someone grabbed me hard and shook me. I blinked, Sadie's bright blue eyes inches away from mine.

"Get out of your head, you hear me?" she shouted in my face. "Wake up and fight!"

Suddenly, all sound returned: screaming, weapons clashing, blood splattering, feet stomping. And in the far distance behind us I heard screams of terror and children crying.

We'd escaped the Woodfaces only to be

reunited with them.

Steadying my breathing, I aimed my crossbow at the leader's face—at the eyehole in his mask—and fired my shot. The bolt shot so fast I didn't even see it leave my weapon. The leader's head shot back, his mask splitting in half, and he collapsed to his knees.

With a thump, he fell sideways, dead.

I looked at Sadie and nodded firmly as a way of saying, "We've got this," and loaded another bolt.

I wasn't about to give up, and I'd die fighting if I had to.

Visit **shadeowens.com** for more works by Shade Owens, including book #4 of The Immortal Ones series.

www.ingramcontent.com/pod-product-compliance
Lightning Source LLC
Chambersburg PA
CBHW032147190726
48290CB00005BB/1442